LUIGI FERRO
BROADCAST MURDER

Luigi Ferro
Broadcast Murder
Copyright © 2023
Cover by Mats Ingelborn.
Photos by A.Karnaushenko, Kiuikson & Wirestock
ISBN print: 978-91-89822-24-5
ISBN e-book: 978-91-89822-25-2
Published by Yabot AB, Sweden, 2023

1

I casted my gaze upon her, a woman named Leila – a troubled soul whose origins traced back to the sun-soaked town of Mesagne in the southern reaches of Puglia. She had traveled far to engage my services, and here, in the confines of my office, her distress had reached a crescendo, manifesting in unrestrained sobs.

My eyes momentarily turned towards the window, revealing a world that had shed its rain-laden burdens. The ceaseless hum of tourist activity outside seemed to dissolve into a distant hum on this fourth-floor enclave. A modest attic office, secured within the heart of San Marino's most prominent square, served as my sanctum. From the vantage point of Piazza della Libertà, the eye was drawn to the commanding presence of the Palazzo Pubblico, the town's administrative core and governmental edifice, and offered a panoramic vista over the valleys below.

Leaning over the expanse of my desk, Leila buried her troubled countenance against her upturned arm. Blonde tresses cascaded over the surface like a curtain of sadness. Her tiny form was barely visible beneath the white T-shirt that covered her slender shoulders. A simple off-the-rack flowery skirt hung from her slim hips. She was in her mid-twenties and had come to seek my help to talk with her older sister. The sister who was on every TV. Marilena Lisa, the name on everyone's lips in San Marino.

I had been too direct and curt with Leila, but speaking softly was not my forte. I shifted uncomfortably in my seat as her eyes filled with tears that spilled onto the stack of papers on my desk. Handling weeping persons did not come naturally to me, particularly women who also were my clients.

So, offering solace, I tried words and broke the silence that lingered like a specter in the room.

"Look, I'll talk to Marilena Lisa, okay?" I said, trying to sound gentle.

She stopped crying but didn't move.

"I'm on it, Leila. I'll find out about her threats."

I moved closer and rested my hand on her fragile shoulder. Her gaze eventually met mine, and I could see the deep sadness in her eyes. Her lips trembled as she spoke, her voice broken by emotion: "Ferro," she whispered, tears glistening in her eyes, "You're the only one I trust. I'm counting on you."

A wry smile tugged at the corner of my lips. "That's what I like to hear," I remarked, a glimmer of levity interwoven with gravity.

A question, a chide, escaped her lips. "Did you have to be so blunt earlier?"

I offered her a steadying hand, coaxing her to rise. She sought refuge in my proximity, her shivering form a testament to the residual storm within her. "No more fear, got it?" I assured softly.

The narrative threads unfolded, and the tapestry of trust woven between us grew stronger.

*

"I need to leave now."

Caterina's announcement sliced through the hum of the taverna, her intent clear—departure was on the horizon, bound for a soiree. Personally, the concept of cocktail parties exuded a certain dismal quality, an abyss into which I had little inclination to plunge. Seated amidst the familiar ambiance of our local taverna, I savored the contents of my wine glass, a nectar worthy of my attention.

"Why leave when the wine's this good?" I mused aloud. A quizzical eyebrow arched as I probed further. "What's so important?"

I looked at her. Her raven-black hair's soft, shiny strands tumbled past her shoulders in perfect waves and framed her heart-shaped face. Her large brown eyes sparkled like freshly polished rocks, and her full lips curved up into a gentle smile. She wore a yellow dress tightly fitted in the chest and waist but flared out at the bottom to a wide skirt that fell just above her knees. Every detail of her outfit was carefully chosen as if she truly belonged in a 1950s French movie.

Caterina noticed my gaze, smiling. Her response, assertive and unwavering, mirrored her resolve. "It's a big deal, darling. It's for Marilena Lisa, and I have to be there."

My gaze locked onto hers. "Marilena Lisa, the television host?"

A nod, laden with a hint of exasperation. "Are there hordes of Marilena Lisas frolicking about, my love?"

Curiosity piqued, and I pressed on. " "Who's throwing this party?"

"None other than Umberto Di Mauro, the grand maestro behind the realms of SMTV."

"SMTV, indeed?" I interjected, a note of disbelief tinging my tone.

San Marino TV was the micro-state's bespoke conduit for radio and televised broadcasts. Within its constellation, Marilena Lisa shone as a fixed star. Her talk show had lured luminaries from both the Italian realm and a broader international stage.

"Indeed," Caterina affirmed. "They're celebrating Marilena's show getting picked up by RAI. Maybe you'll watch it if you ever get a TV."

Implicit within her words danced a suggestion, a playful jest—my disinterest in contemporary affairs and technology was a recurrent trope. Though hardly revolutionary, televisions had never found a niche within my abode. Still, I couldn't feign ignorance when it came to Marilena's show; fragments of her interviews and performances had graced my senses. An elegant figure she was, possessed of cascading blonde locks, statuesque stature, and a poise that stirred envy in any woman. Her allure transcended the screen.

"Bellissima," I murmured, thoughts escaping me momentarily.

"Who are you talking about?" A dangerous glint ignited Caterina's dark eyes.

A casual shrug accompanied the draining of my wine glass. "Just the beauty of the moment."

Reality reasserted itself, as did Caterina's purpose. "So, I have to get going."

Her words propelled us into action; I left a ten Euro

note on the table, nodding gratitude to Fabio, the taverna's owner. "Time to seize the night," I uttered, donning an air of readiness.

Caterina rose, her features a portrait of mild astonishment. "Luigi, were you even invited?"

My reply was nonchalant. "Does it matter?" As her hand took hold of my arm, I was drawn closer, her proximity enveloping me.

"I shall be honored to accompany you," she cooed.

"Where's this thing?"

"Within a villa in Faetano," Caterina shared, her smile warm. "Not too far, my love."

My Vespa hummed to life beneath me, its engine's rumble a familiar cadence. She settled behind me, her embrace snug, her dress granting a tantalizing glimpse of her thighs.

The night beckoned, and we set forth.

*

Amidst the tumult of that crowded garden, she remained a distinct figure, effortlessly capturing attention. A fixture of television exposure had bestowed upon her countenance a familiarity matched only by the moon. Not to mention, the glossy Italian magazines and the daily broadsheets carried her image with unerring regularity.

Marilena Lisa, the tall, beautiful, unnatural blonde who perched atop a pedestal while the world craned its neck to catch a fleeting glimpse of her. A creature often dubbed a Nordic maiden, conjured from the pages of ancient Scandinavian sagas. While her Nordic lineage and maidenhood claims might be a stretch, the reality of her beauty held true. Stature was her canvas; at the garden soiree within Di Mauro's opulent villa, she transcended the evening, a beacon piercing the revelry sea. Her blue dress was so tight it would have revealed every extra gram on her body if there had been one. A plunging neckline designed to show off her enhanced upper assets and a hemline short enough to set her well-sculptured legs in focus.

Whispers swirled, asserting that her next season's contract had commanded a sum surpassing a million Euros. Marilena Lisa, her name echoing like an incantation.

"Exquisite!" murmured the man behind me, his voice carrying a breath of awe. "As beautiful as a fashion model, but with intelligence to match."

The compact congregation seemed intent on swaying like reeds in a current. I navigated through the human tide to reach the bar. Caterina's silhouette waved like a reassuring lighthouse. I seized two drinks and made my course toward her.

"Luigi... I had feared you'd vanish in the crowd!"

The man beside her smiled, perpetually affable. The kind whose grin was ever-present. Taller than most, impeccably garbed in a three-piece linen suit, his shirt gleaming white, accented by a red tie. Gray, hinting at the wisdom of years, grazed his temples, and his clean-shaven countenance bore the patina of sun-kissed skin.

"Luigi, let me introduce Umberto Di Mauro."

The handshake he offered crushed my hand, a display

of strength that verged on the extreme. "Luigi Ferro, a pleasure to have you with us."

"A grand party, Signore."

"Managed to get something to drink?"

"Yep, and one for Caterina as well."

The chalice of white wine was delivered to her, and we saluted the host with a clink.

Di Mauro's eyes returned to me, a smile etched in his expression. "She's remarkable, isn't she?"

"Absolutely," I concurred. "Signora Lisa is indeed a captivating sight. A sight for sore eyes."

He chuckled softly, his hand finding its place upon Caterina's shoulder. "You misunderstand, Ferro. My focus was not on Marilena. I meant Caterina. She is my cherished one. I've been striving to coax her into doing more for me than presenting the weather. I'd like her to take over after Marilena, but she remains resolute in her resistance..."

"Maybe she's busy with other stuff?" I suggested.

The night's narrative continued to weave, a tapestry threaded with conversations and enigmas.

His gaze lingered upon me, penetrating as though searching for answers within my depths. An enigmatic smile graced his lips again, but his words stumbled mid-course.

"I didn't mean..." He halted himself, a fleeting glimpse of vulnerability. "Never mind. I've got other guests to attend to. Enjoy the party."

He departed, his head held aloft, a projection of self-assurance.

"Does he think Marilena Lisa belongs to him?" I asked Caterina.

"Don't make her sound like property," she shot back.

"So, is he your boss too?"

Amusement spilled forth from her lips, her wine glass brought to the brink of her smile.

"Well, Di Mauro's a big deal, wouldn't you say?"

"He's the media king of San Marino. Remind me, and I'll get you some articles to read up on. There are probably enough press clippings to keep you occupied over the coming year."

I dodged her question. "What's his deal with Lisa?"

"Why this ceaseless curiosity, Luigi?" Caterina's gaze locked onto mine, her glass lowered. "Between us, though, he's got a thing for Marilena."

"Really?"

"Crazy for her," Caterina reiterated, a furrow forming between her obsidian eyes. "What makes a guy act like that?"

"You asking for my expert opinion?"

"You get what I mean. Di Mauro acts like a lovesick teenager around her, captivated by Marilena."

"Maybe it's good for business?"

Caterina's shrug embodied nonchalance. "Even if he hated her, she'd still be a star."

"Is he married?"

"No, he's a widower," she said, looking away for a moment. "Marilena's been married twice, though."

"I can well imagine," I quipped, a grin accompanying my words. "She's got the whole country lining up."

"Her last husband was singer Franco Marini. Ever heard of him?" She prodded me with a playful nudge.

"Yes," I responded, sidestepping her bait. "And before him, her first husband, Umberto Bortoloni, met an untimely end."

She blinked, her gaze sharpening upon me. "Luigi Ferro, you surprise me. When did you start reading the gossip column?"

A shift in the atmosphere, a whisper of movement.

"She approaches," I remarked.

Caterina gasped, her gaze deliberately averted.

"Marilena?"

"You said there's only one," I retorted. "A friend of yours?"

"I don't have many friends here."

"Except a special one, right?"

A sheepish smile graced her lips, an unexpected charm.

"Oh, Luigi... you mean you?"

A voice materialized from behind me, a lament painting the words. "I've spent the evening conversing with dreary strangers. My old comrades have forsaken me."

And there she stood, a vision of elegance, a living statue wrapped in a form-fitting dress that dared to leave little to the imagination. Diamonds glinted like stars around her neck and ears.

Bellissima.

"Marilena, you look amazing," Caterina uttered, her smile holding a calculated edge. "Lovely to see you again."

"Darling!" Marilena's address was thrown Caterina's way without a direct glance. Instead, those inquisitive navy-blue eyes fixed their gaze upon me.

Caterina took it upon herself to clarify. "This is Luigi Ferro."

Marilena's smile stirred memories of a drowsy tigress.

"The detective?" she asked.

"A fact you ought to be aware of," I responded.

"Should I?" Her smile wavered.

"I guess this party just got interesting for you," Caterina hissed indignantly, swiveling away to greet other acquaintances.

"Well, well," I mused. "Permit me to get you a drink."

Marilena's head swayed a slow negative.

"Not for me," she announced. "I prefer mineral water, nothing stronger."

"Kudos to your restraint," I quipped, savoring the last of my wine.

My trajectory led me back towards the bar for a real drink, and Marilena followed in measured steps. The chilled glass of gin with a slice of lime in my hand beckoned to her, and we gravitated towards a more secluded enclave within the garden. Despite the nearness of laughter and conversations from the assembled guests, an almost palpable boundary seemed to divide us from the rest. A subtle aura of pine trees enveloped us, a fragrance I embraced with satisfaction. The heavy perfumes that often suffused such gatherings were hardly to my liking.

"So, you thought I should know you?" Marilena Lisa began, her tone bearing a hint of impatience.

"Know me, you say?" I countered, a wry grin shaping my lips.

"Indeed, Signore. You presumed I should recognize you, know what you are. Do you think you're famous, that I should have read about you in the papers?"

"Not at all," I responded, my tone firm. "In my view, nobody should be reading stories of crime and misdeeds. Our world already swims in a sea of transgressions."

"Ferro, spare me the mystery!" Marilena's gaze held mine, a silent appraisal.

"Sorry, no more games," I said, a playful note coloring my words. "You're right; games are best suited for children, perhaps those who played at the old water mill in Zegno di Puglia, west of Mesagne? Sisters like Maria and Leila Luca?"

A spark ignited within her eyes, a flame unfamiliar yet captivating, as she locked her gaze onto mine, her breath held in suspension.

The rim of my glass met my lips, but fate intervened, causing a slip.

"You must've been cute as a kid, braces and all," I said, raising my glass to her. "To the memory of Maria Luca, the girl from Zegno di Puglia, a village of three thousand."

"Stop it," she hissed, her words a seething command. She took measured steps toward me, proximity filling the space with her perfume, her allure almost intoxicating. "How much do you want for your silence?"

"Ask your sister; she's the one paying," I retorted.

"Enough of this," she whispered, her voice hoarse yet charged with ferocity. Head tilted back, lips parted, revealing her pristine teeth that gleamed like pearls. "I knew she would find you, or someone like you..."

"You keeping tabs on her?"

"We need to talk," she declared, evading my query.

"I'm listening, my dear."

"Not here."

I extended one of my cards toward her. "Here's how to find me."

She sized me up, her gaze probing, a testament to her stature that brought our eyes almost level. "Could you manage a meeting tomorrow?"

"Sure." My response was accompanied by a nonchalant shrug.

"I'm busy all day, and we're taping our last show in the evening. But afterward, I'll be available. How about you join the audience?"

"I'll be there."

"SMTV studio, nine o'clock. After that, we could perhaps dine together and talk..."

"You're making it sound rather serious."

She replied with a smile, a blend of ease and control. "Blackmail, too, is a serious matter."

"If you've got nothing to hide, you've got nothing to worry about," I said and met her gaze squarely. "Especially from a younger sister."

"My past doesn't trouble me! Yet, I want to leave it behind."

"Not my concern," I declared.

"So you're on Leila's side, looking for a payout to keep quiet?"

"Leila's had two close calls," I recounted. "First in

Zegno di Puglia, then in Rimini. A third one might not go so well. The police will have to be involved. See you tomorrow."

I was about to depart when Umberto Di Mauro's imposing presence barreled through the crowd. His exclamation rang out in his characteristic, exaggerated manner.

"Ferro, monopolizing our guest of honor? I must protest."

"Please, feel free," I retorted. "She's all yours."

Navigating the sea of onlookers' glares, I forged a path to the grand iron gate leading to the street. Just as I reached it, a faint echo of footsteps reached my ears. Caterina appeared, her breath slightly uneven. You could've said goodbye."

"Si, naturally. Goodbye, honey."

"Luigi Ferro... Do you always have to be like that? I hate it!"

"Honey," I mused, stepping through the gate. A hiss of fury followed, and Caterina's presence lingered as she followed me into the obscurity of the street.

"I'll come with you," she murmured.

"It's a free country," I responded with a shrug.

Silently, we walked in tandem to where my Vespa was parked. As I retrieved the helmet from its hook, Caterina grabbed my arm. "Luigi... what happened between you and Marilena? I saw you, the intense focus you shared."

"Love at first sight," I said with a wink.

"Luigi, darling." The cute dimples on her tanned cheeks deepened as she smiled. "What if we went somewhere... just the two of us... and enjoyed dinner?"

"Absolutely."

"You don't sound too excited," she teased, her hand lightly resting on my chest. "How about my place? We'd be alone and..."

I regarded her, her voice carrying an undercurrent.

"You're trying to get Marilena's secrets out of me." I stated.

"But darling?!"

"My place or nowhere," I said, cutting her off.

2

I emerged from the shower, enveloped in a green patterned towel.

"I'll fetch you another drink," I stated, navigating my way toward the kitchen.

The chime of the doorbell reverberated through the space.

My gaze swept the room, capturing Caterina's nude silhouette sprawled on the couch. She kindled a cigarette, tendrils of smoke curling towards the ceiling.

A sole beacon of light emanated from a candle ensconced in a grand brass candlestick—a memento gifted to me by my mother upon my graduation.

Turning towards the door, I noted Caterina's hushed query, "Late-night visitors, Luigi?"

"Probably a delivery guy or my nosy neighbor," I surmised. "You'd better stay out of sight; he doesn't like brunettes."

Her suppressed chuckle reached my ears as I approached the entrance. As my hand gripped the doorknob, a distinct signal sounded.

Cracking the door a few inches, a mellifluous voice inquired, "Is Signor Luigi Ferro here?"

Parting the door wider, I observed a figure in the corridor. Clad in a coat, a flat cap perched askew, the man bore a fragile demeanor.

"Can we talk, Signor Ferro?"

"Not now."

"Are you alone?"

"I'm busy," I began, preparing to conclude the interaction. However, he interjected, placing his foot within the threshold.

"Don't do that," I warned. "You're welcome at my office tomorrow, and we'll talk business."

"I need to talk now," he retorted, his hand emerging from his coat pocket; a fleeting glint of metal caught my eye.

Freeing his foot, I extended a begrudging invitation, "Va bene. If it must be this way..."

Crossing the threshold, he entered my domain, and seizing the opportunity, I slammed the door forcefully. Yet, his reflexes proved quicker, my momentum only briefly pinning him, his firearm discharging with a subdued thud. A twitch of the towel around me and instinct urged me away from the door-frame. Pain radiated from my hip, my attention caught by his entry.

Recollection reminded me of my firearm resting upon the coffee table, a relic from our disrobed state.

A fleeting glimpse captured his unassuming countenance. Leaping beyond the couch, I lunged for the gun on the table, awareness dawning that my chances were scant. Even as I rose with the automatic in hand, his looming figure surpassed my peripheral vision, his gun held low, reminiscent of gangsters from bygone films.

The muffled pop of his silenced firearm punctuated the air, and a shroud descended upon my senses. Everything went black. I didn't see Caterina grab the brass candlestick and swing.

*

"Oh, Luigi, you're alive!"

I pried open my other eye, adjusting to the room's illumination.

"Ease that pressure off my head," I requested.

Caterina's voice carried a tremor of relief. "There's no weight on your head, darling. It's just a damp towel…"

My hand gingerly met my forehead, peeling away the towel. A cacophony akin to twenty turbines at full throttle roared inside my skull.

Recollection struck—a door, a man. Struggling to rise, Caterina's grip held me back. Anxiety etched her features, and I inquired, "Where's the guy with the gun?"

"He's gone. I hit him with the candlestick."

"You did what?"

"As he took a shot at you, I bashed him in the back of his head with your hefty candlestick."

I managed to ascend to a seated posture.

The brass candlestick stood solitary on the coffee table, its candle extinguished and wax speckled around.

"Could you fetch me a drink?" I asked.

"Of course. There's water right here."

"Gin with a slice of lime would be preferred," I asserted.

"If that's your preference?"

"Not just a preference; it's what I need."

As she retreated to the kitchen, I noticed she had redressed, though her hair remained tousled. A cautious appraisal revealed my injuries—my left ear and temple grazed by the bullet.

"Lucky," I mused.

Caterina, standing a distance away, met my gaze and smiled.

"He fired twice, and you get just a scratch."

"My life insurance company will celebrate this," I quipped, rising and surveying the surroundings. "Alright, honey. Tell me what happened?"

"Exactly as I told you," she replied, handing me the gin. "I struck him, and he wavered but didn't topple. He seemed quite surprised by my presence. Then he turned and left, leaving the door wide open..."

As I drained the glass, she looked at me, concern etched on her features. I handed her the empty glass. "A refill, perhaps?"

"Ah, Luigi! I'm so glad you're okay,"

"Let's not get carried away," I responded, following her to the kitchen.

Observing her replenish the glass, I voiced my gratitude. "Thanks for helping me."

A bashful smile graced her lips. "You've helped me before. You'll do it again."

"You're my good luck charm," I remarked, punctuating it with a swift kiss.

Surveying my unclothed form and the hip wound, I noted Caterina had tended to it, skillfully patching it up.

"So you had to undress me again?" I teased.

"I had to treat the wound. I was worried you wouldn't wake up. I almost called a doctor or the police..."

"Police?" I echoed, savoring the gin. "Caterina, you're quite the remarkable woman."

"Thank you," she purred.

"You're probably the sole lady in this town who'd take on a gunman with a candlestick and not call for backup."

"I thought you'd want to keep it quiet," she said. "You know, because of your job."

"This isn't an everyday thing," I remarked, finishing the last drops in my glass. "I'm gonna clean up."

I headed to the bathroom, with her trailing behind, her figure leaning against the door-frame. I inspected the mirror as the water cascaded into the sink, contemplating the scratch along my left temple. After a time, I shifted my focus to her. Her full lips curled into a mischievous smile.

"Well," I remarked, "I could use some help here, or maybe a nurse."

"Don't blame yourself for that guy," she reassured. Her voice held a soothing note.

"I wish you'd hit him harder," I mused. Making my way to the bedroom, I donned a fresh shirt from the dresser. Returning to the living room, I spotted my trousers on the floor, half-concealed beneath the couch. I poured another glass of wine for Caterina, gesturing for her to relax and take it easy.

Abruptly, she stirred and drew a sharp breath. "Luigi, I forgot—he left his gun behind."

My gaze fixed on her. "Where?"

"Over there," she gestured toward the window. "I kicked it as he dropped it."

I picked up the firearm, meticulously examining it. It was a 9mm Browning. Committing the serial number to memory, I retrieved my phone and initiated a call to the police.

While awaiting Mateo Capparoni's response, Caterina voiced her concern. "I thought you didn't want to involve the police?"

"He's not just any cop."

A gruff "Pronto" resonated from the phone, but for assurance, I inquired, "Is this Comandante Capparoni?"

"Speaking! Though to be correct, it's the Vice Comandante."

"Alright, Vice Comandante," I sighed. "It's Luigi Ferro."

"What prompted this honor?" Capparoni queried. "It's been a while..."

"Can you do me a favor? I need to trace the owner of a weapon through Italy's registry."

"Is it a handgun?"

"It's not a missile," I quipped.

"Fine, text me the number, and I'll see what I can unearth."

After describing the Browning and forwarding the number, he posed a follow-up question. "How urgent is this? Do you realize how many Brownings are registered?"

"At the moment, I'm not that concerned with statistics, Capparoni," I replied. "However, if you could find the owner of this weapon, you'd be doing me a great favor."

"Fine, but you owe me one," he retorted, his tone carrying authority.

"Name it," I responded.

A sardonic chuckle echoed through the line.

"Va bene," I responded evenly. "Who should I expect the call from?"

"I'll have one of my guys reach out to you," he said, adding, "Where'd you find the gun?"

"A stranger left it for me on the floor."

"You're joking, right?"

"Yes, can't you hear the humor in my voice?"

"What's the actual story behind this?" Capparoni's tone grew serious.

"I'll fill you in tomorrow. I might manage to extract some fingerprints from the weapon for your team to analyze."

"This is getting interesting," Capparoni commented. "Has someone tried to kill you?"

"They can always try," I replied. "This one caught me off guard. I'm unsure about his identity or motives. What I do know is he was resolute. He discharged two rounds, yet I emerged with barely a scratch."

"You're quite a lucky fool," Capparoni muttered. "When did this happen?"

"An hour or so ago."

"And the guy got away?"

"Well, he's not keeping me company. I blacked out after that second shot."

"You've certainly had an eventful night."

"You have no idea," I agreed. "By the way, the gun had a silencer."

There was a brief pause on Capparoni's end.

"You should probably describe the guy."

"What's in it for me?"

"Damn it!" Capparoni's voice brimmed with frustration. "Don't you want this man apprehended?"

"I was thinking of handling it myself."

"Only to risk your private investigator's license by declining cooperation with law enforcement. Ferro, the Gendarmerie, is intrigued by characters like your mysterious stranger. We want to catch people like this."

"Okay, fine," I acquiesced, eyeing the gun on the kitchen sink. I hadn't disturbed the silencer—it appeared loose and out of function.

"Don't get too excited about this," I continued. " The guy was about five feet, thin, clean-shaven. Didn't catch his hair color."

Capparoni mused, "It could still be useful. You never know."

I sensed him hastily jotting down my account. So I remarked, "He wore a beige coat and a soft flat cap, perhaps gray."

"Grazie, Luigi."

"No problem. But don't forget to examine the Browning."

I terminated the call and shifted my attention to Caterina. She regarded me intently.

"Luigi," she began suddenly, "I had a thought."

"Uh-huh?" I responded, gingerly holding the gun by its silencer, placing it on the coffee table, illuminating the room, and fetching fingerprint powder and a camera.

"Luigi, what if that guy has something to do with your talk with Marilena Lisa?"

I glanced at her. "Let me worry about that. I don't want you getting hurt."

"Luigi?!" she exclaimed with a snarl. "I could be onto something or at least on the right path."

I remained silent as she observed me, meticulously

applying fine dust across the firearm's surface. Afterward, I gently brushed off the excess with a soft brush.

”I see fingerprints!” she declared.

”Those might very well be yours,” I pointed out as I lifted the camera. She fell into silence for a moment.

”Aren't you going to say anything?” She finally broke the stillness. ”After all, I did save your life!”

”As you wish,” I sighed. ”Get us a drink while I finish up here.”

”Only if you promise to tell...”

”Yes, yes,” I interjected. ”Just chill until I finish this.”

I documented the evidence through photographs and stashed the fingerprinting materials before securing the Browning in a drawer. A glass of red wine awaited me, and I grasped it, commencing my narrative.

”About a week ago, a woman named Leila Luca visited my office,” I began. ”She claimed to be from Zegno di Puglia, a small village near Mesagne. She introduced herself as Marilena Lisa's sister.”

Caterina audibly caught her breath, her surprise evident. I turned to regard her.

”Keep it to yourself, honey,” I warned. ”This is serious stuff, almost a sensational revelation.”

”Do I need to use the candlestick on you too?” she retorted with indignation. ”Watch yourself, Luigi Ferro. My right arm swing is not to be played with...”

”Easy,” I said, raising my hands in mock defense. ”Perhaps I don't need to remind you to keep this quiet. But I won't hesitate to dig further into Lisa's history. There's more beneath the surface.”

”Puglia!” Caterina exclaimed, her voice laced with

surprise. "So, that's her place of origin. People have been speculating for ages. Some thought she hailed from Scandinavia, and I've heard..."

"Want the full story or not?" I cut in. "Or shall we engage in a cozy round of gossip?"

"Sorry, Luigi," she conceded, shifting to the far end of the couch and tucking her slender legs underneath her. Her endearing charm was enough to make anyone swoon—I certainly had.

I refilled my wine glass and continued, "Leila Luca is a charming young woman in her mid-twenties who looks nothing like Marilena. There's something about her that exudes a rustic charm, like that of a village girl. You'd probably say her fashion sense is outdated or even tasteless. She resides in a tranquil apartment complex, where she's lived since her parents passed away five years ago. She holds a position as a clerk at the City Council. She has no male companions and is a devoted churchgoer, attending service every Sunday."

"So she's the opposite of Marilena," Caterina sighed.

"Exactly," I affirmed. "Marilena, too, was once a village girl, just like her sister. But she cast that life aside upon her marriage to Umberto Bortoloni."

"Ah, yes," Caterina mused. "Umberto Bortoloni, her first husband—the elusive man no one has seen!"

"He won't be seen again," I continued, my tone unwavering. "Umberto Bortoloni, he's dead. He owned a big transport company in Bari. He was a widower with no offspring, well over two decades senior to Marilena. At the time, she was employed at a beauty salon and was renowned in the town for her striking looks."

Caterina leaned forward, her posture attuned and her senses fully engaged. She was the ideal audience.

"How old was Marilena then?" Caterina inquired.

"She was around nineteen," I responded, "and Leila a few years her junior. Their parents were in dire straits, and when the affluent widower slipped a ring onto Marilena's finger, it was seen as a monumental feat for the family. Unfortunately, the union didn't endure beyond the first year."

"What happened to him?" Caterina asked.

"He caught a cold, developed pneumonia, and it was a swift descent into death."

A hush draped the room for a moment. I leaned forward, placing the glass back on the table. "Marilena left town after his funeral. She inherited a significant sum from Bortoloni, but he had a sizeable family, and her marriage to him wasn't exactly embraced by them. Following his death, numerous legal wranglings emerged, but Leila didn't know all the details. She thinks Marilena didn't receive as much from the estate as she should have."

"So she married him for the money?" Caterina queried.

"What else?" I responded with a casual shrug. "According to Leila, Bortoloni wasn't exactly Prince Charming. Overweight, balding, a heavy drinker, and fixated on financial gains. Started as a truck driver, ended up owning the biggest trucking company in the Puglia region."

"Interesting," Caterina mused. "I can almost see him

before me. But what happened with Marilena after his death?"

"You don't expect me to present her entire career résumé, do you?" A sweet smile crossed Caterina's face as she shook her head. I continued, "She migrated north, started as a hostess—first at trade shows and conventions—then found a role at a radio station in Bologna. It was there she encountered her second spouse, the singer Franco Marini. Following their divorce, she was approached with an offer at SMTV, and the rest, as they say, is history. Though, I suspect her PR manager Sonia Masco or her agent Renato Scarpa could provide a more detailed curriculum vitae."

"Clearly, you've done your homework on Marilena Lisa," Caterina noted.

"Of course," I affirmed. "I've certainly learnt alot in the past couple of days."

"Why did you choose to dig into this?" Caterina questioned.

"I'd be equally intrigued to learn why you connected that guy to Marilena Lisa," I countered.

"Let's call it feminine intuition," Caterina chimed in.

I regarded her with an expression that communicated my thoughts on that statement.

"Leila Luca came to me really concerned," I said. "She had this peaceful life going on in Zegno di Puglia, and then out of nowhere, she gets this anonymous letter telling her to stay away from her sister—or something bad would happen. Then she gets another letter, same creepy vibe. A box of chocolates shows up after that. Leila thought it was from the assistant pastor, who's been showing interest in her for a while. She takes a bite, but it tastes off, so she spits it out. Her dog eats it and ends up dying a painful death. It's a mess."

"Good heavens!" Caterina exclaimed, horrified. "I thought such macabre things only happened in movies."

"That's how it is," I said. "Someone could've seen an vintage crime movie and thought poisoning chocolates was a good idea. A potent poison remains an effective means of eliminating undesirable individuals. Just inject some poison into each chocolate piece."

Caterina let out a shudder of disbelief. "That's twisted!"

"Leila Luca was lucky," I proceeded. "After her dog died, Leila first thought she just got some bad chocolates, like they were expired or something. She didn't even talk about it until one day the topic of spoiled food came up. That's when she finally went to the police. By then, though, she'd thrown the rest of the chocolates away, so the cops didn't have any evidence to go on."

Caterina grabbed her pack of cigarettes, and I flicked the lighter for her. "The more you talk, the less I'm feeling for Marilena. Are you saying she deliberately kept her distance from her little sister and pretended not to know her or something?"

"Keep in mind, Puglia is quite distant from here," I interjected. "Leila resided there while Marilena was here. They maintained no contact, and though many in Zegno di Puglia knew Marilena Lisa's origins and true identity, they remained silent."

"It's not unusual for accomplished individuals to hide their pasts," Caterina reflected, offering a nod of understanding.

"Indeed. Leila didn't tell the cops about the letters because she didn't want to make trouble for Marilena," I explained. "She still looks up to her, even though Marilena refuses to see her."

"What?!" Caterina burst out, her hands gesturing vehemently, causing her cigarette to tumble to the floor.

"Steady," I remarked, retrieving the fallen cigarette and tapping the ash into the tray. "Marilena could have her reasons for avoiding Leila, whatever they may be. Leila stayed at a rather rundown hotel en route to Rimini for about two weeks. During that time, she attempted to reach out to Marilena roughly ten times, all to no avail."

Caterina's curiosity sparkled in her gaze. "Why did she come to you, Luigi? Was it due to the attempts on her life?"

"There was a second incident after her arrival," I affirmed, my head tilting slowly. "If it were anyone besides Leila, it might have appeared purely accidental. She was standing near the hotel entrance, and at the very moment, a truck laden with barrels—beer kegs, in fact—appeared on the scene..."

"Kegs?" Caterina interjected, seeking clarification.

"Yes, those metallic beer containers," I clarified. "In any case, it seemed the truck was heading straight for the hotel entrance. Just as it reached her, one of the kegs... barrels... toppled from the truck and crashed onto the street, mere centimeters away. The impact knocked her unconscious, but she sustained no serious injuries. When she woke up, the truck was gone, just the hefty barrel behind."

Caterina repositioned herself on the couch, her posture more at ease. "So it could've just been an accident?"

"Could be," I conceded. "Leila was in a near-hysterical state upon awakening, and the police escorted her to the station. She provided a statement, recounting the entire episode, yet I suspect they didn't fully buy her story."

Caterina's expression remained inquisitive. "Her story must've sounded weird."

"Exactly," I confirmed. "Talking about poisoned chocolates and plummeting kegs... The police likely chalked it up to confusion."

"So she sought your help," Caterina deduced, her tone contemplative.

"She found me online and got in touch," I revealed. "She shared her story bit by bit, though I had to press for all the details. She hesitated to implicate Marilena—the famous star must be shielded at any cost."

"And what can Luigi Ferro do for the frightened girl from Puglia?"

"I might be able to figure out who's blackmailing Marilena."

"What?" Caterina exclaimed, her astonishment evident. "Blackmail against Marilena! But you haven't..."

"I can't reveal everything just yet, honey," I responded. "I'm still piecing it together. But it looks like Marilena thinks Leila is behind the blackmail, which is why she won't see her."

*

After a string of exchanged words and a cigarette's worth of time, Caterina voiced her thoughts. "This whole situation is a tangled mess, or perhaps my brain has simply called it a night."

"It has indeed been quite the evening," I conceded, rising from my seat and beginning to pace the room. "Leila's gotten two more threats since she got here, both as texts from a number that can't be traced. The person's watching her. The latest threats even told her to stop asking anything from Marilena, or she'd end up in the Adriatic Sea, wearing cement shoes instead of flip-flops."

Caterina gasped, her eyes wide with horror. "That's awful!"

"Blackmail rarely comes with a touch of finesse," I quipped, a wry smile tugging at my lips. "And the same can be said about murder."

I cast a glance at the clock. "It's getting late," I remarked, extending my hand toward her. She took it, allowing me to pull her to her feet.

She pressed herself against me, tilting her head back. "Is there anything else you're not telling me, Luigi?"

"I've told you most of it," I responded with a yawn. "My starting point is Marilena's blackmail situation."

Caterina blushed, moistening her lips. "Luigi, you have to help her."

As I remained silent, she persisted, her expression earnest. "You can't let anything harmful befall that poor girl. You must get in touch with the authorities and—"

"I'm already on it," I interjected. "I went to that party with you as an excuse to see Marilena. I've seen her on TV, but never met her in person before."

"You'll probably see her again," Caterina remarked, her brow furrowing. "I can't picture her as anything other than her TV self. But who's sending those threats? Leila?"

An eyebrow of mine arched at her supposition. "It's possible..."

Her voice lowered to a whisper. "Or perhaps it's Marilena..."

"Could be her too," I agreed. "I did tell Marilena that Leila had contacted me. Your hunch about the guy who showed up tonight with a Browning, potentially connected to Marilena, isn't bad at all. What I need now, however, is solid proof."

3

The phone began its persistent ring as I stood enveloped in the morning shower's embrace. Swiftly, I reached for a towel, my dripping silhouette darting into the bedroom to answer the insistent call.

"Pronto!"

"Luigi? It's Silvano Ghia."

"Uhu?" I responded, feigning ignorance.

"Your old mate Silvano, remember? News, first but not least."

Silvano Ghia's voice matched his substantial frame. He was a reporter at the local paper La Tribuna Oggi.

"Alright, Ghia," I muttered, "I'm getting myself sorted."

With a playful tap on Caterina's bare behind, I roused her from her slumber. As she stirred, I indicated that it was time to rise. Slipping into the shirt from the previous night, I took the call in the kitchen.

"So, what's this about, Silvano?"

"I saw you at Umberto Di Mauro's party last night," he said. "We were at opposite ends of the garden, but I noticed you have a tête-à-tête with none other than La Lisa herself! What's the deal, Luigi? Are you joining her fan club?"

"Been a fan for a while," I fabricated.

"So, you're into high society now?" he prodded. When I remained silent, he carried on. "I've never seen you at an event like that, Luigi. It's not like you to be at these events, especially talking to Marilena Lisa with…"

"Have you got a question, or are we just chatting?" I interjected, my patience wearing thin. "I'm in the midst of something here."

"A question? Oh, right," he replied, his tone perplexed.

A sigh of frustration escaped my lips. "Silvano, I'll owe you a drink…"

"Now? It's rather early, isn't it?"

"Later," I clarified. "Right now, I'm busy."

"Can't give me anything now?" he persisted. "Is there a case tied to Di Mauro's television studio? Or perhaps it's linked to Marilena Lisa?"

"Didn't you see that I entered and exited the party in the company of Caterina Curiale?" I inquired.

He took the bait, hook, line, and sinker.

"Caterina? Is that why you mingled with the upper crust?"

"Why not?"

"I'm not sure what to make of this," Silvano admitted. "Caterina, you say?"

"Exactly. It could be some fresh fodder for your gossip column: A little sunshine over the Weathergirl and the P.I."

His laughter echoed on the line. "Bene, bene. You're giving me a runaround, but it's not every day I get a quote from Luigi Ferro."

"Talk later, Silvano."

"Aspetta, just a moment…"

I terminated the call.

Taking my time getting dressed, I savored the prospect

of a promising day ahead. The sun was shining, and I had much on my mind. A desperate young woman as my client, an intruding and trigger-happy man, and a TV star on her way to national stardom.

Donning a white shirt and pairing it with a blue linen suit, I appreciated the world of fashion, and given my recent brush with celebrities, I invested an extra effort. I was venturing into the realm of Marilena Lisa. Yet, my allegiance was with my client, Leila Luca, who had entrusted me with her savings to seek justice. Though the compensation held value, my true drive was to put a halt to the harm intended for her.

Time wasn't a luxury I could squander.

*

I swung by the Gendarmerie, the states militarized law enforcement agency. Comandante Capparoni had yet to make his entrance, given his late-night hours. A strapping young cop, built like a professional bodybuilder, entered the waiting room. His blue shirt stretched taut across his chest, and bulging biceps seemed on the brink of rupture. He introduced himself as Petrelli.

"You're the one who sent us those fingerprint photos for identification, right?"

"Yeah," I confirmed.

"We're working on them now."

"Good."

He scrutinized me. "How have you become chummy with the big shot?"

"Capparoni? Who knows? Maybe he's got a thing for my fashion sense..."

"That's one way to put it," Petrelli deadpanned. He pulled out a slip of paper from his pocket and unfurled it.

"The owner of the Browning has been ID'd, Signor Ferro."

"Go on," I prompted, veiling my surprise.

"Maybe you want to write it down?"

"Sure thing," I acquiesced, grabbing an envelope and a pen.

He began a deliberate recitation: "Registered owner of the automatic pistol: Enzo Scavolini. He appears clean, Signor Ferro. He works over at Carlino Transport. They're situated on Strada Dei Censiti. Need the exact address?"

I shook my head. "No need."

"I took the liberty of looking him up, Signor Ferro. I've had a word with his manager."

"Did you ask if Scavolini lost his gun recently?"

"No, I didn't."

I nodded.

"Alright, thank you," I said, slipping the envelope into my pocket. "I guess you didn't get a physical description of Scavolini from his boss?"

"Yes... and no," he hesitated. "I didn't go into details. I thought I'd wait for more facts."

The sardonic undertone in his voice didn't escape me. I offered him a nugget of wisdom: "Maybe Capparoni didn't tell you, but this is my case, Petrelli."

"I wouldn't have expected anything less from your line of work, Signor Ferro," he shot back, emphasizing Signor.

"Don't strain that brain of yours too hard," I retorted before making my exit.

My course led me down the narrow streets that wound through Montegiardino each crooked alleyway a slice of history in its own right. Each ancient house was timeworn, their walls a testament to the centuries, they had stood against wind and weather. At last, I arrived at Scarpa Talenti, the artist agency which managed the bright, shining star Marilena Lisa. The polished glass doors shone in the light of the midday sun.

Behind the reception desk sat a woman with blue hair.

"Si?" Her voice rang sharp and tense.

"Renato Scarpa," I announced. "I'm Luigi Ferro."

She ran her fingers through azure locks. "I'm sorry, but Dottore Scarpa is busy, Signor..."

"Ferro," I reiterated. "Please let him know I'm here."

"Why?"

I leaned in over the counter, and she instinctively pulled back in her chair.

"Why are you wasting your talent here?" I asked with a grin. "A woman like you should be under the spotlight in films... You've got potential. Is Scarpa really that exceptional?"

"Magari!" she exclaimed, casting her eyes downward. "Il Dottore treats us office girls like furniture. Was your name Luigi Ferrous?"

"Ferro," I corrected.

A smile broke through, and as she reached for the phone, I caught a glimpse of her upper attributes.

"Signor Luigi Ferro is here to see you. Are you available?"

There was a muffled response I couldn't make out, and then she cupped the microphone and informed me, "He's heard of you."

"Yes," I affirmed. "We exchanged words on the phone."

Removing her hand from the microphone, she relayed, "Yes, now! Thank you, Dottore."

As she hung up, she rose and ambled toward a distant door. Taller and more svelte than my initial perception, she leaned in as she opened the door, a hint of perfume wafting my way.

"Signor Ferro, Dottore Scarpa."

I cautiously advanced across the expansive office, my steps muffled by the plush carpeting. I reached a desk that seemed to take up a quarter of the room. Behind it sat an overweight man in a rumpled suit, his eyes glued to the laptop before him.

The rotund man paid no heed to my approach. A glass bottle of sparkling mineral water and a case of Alka-Seltzer tablets sat beside it, and every spare inch of wall space was crowded with framed photos and posters—film stars, musicians, famous writers – all smiling down at me.

After a moment, he glanced up from his laptop, seized a pen, and snapped, "Ferro, you're pushing my patience! First, you call and demand my top client names, and now you barge in here, commandeering my precious time."

"Exactly," I responded. "As I informed you, I represent a client getting harassed by some anonymous pest. To advance the case, I require handwriting samples from the artists I mentioned over the phone."

His astonishment registered subtly, followed by a lean back in his chair, his gaze fixed on me.

"Handwriting? What the hell for?" he erupted.

"My client has received written threats naming Giuseppe Fazio, Marilena Lisa, and Mario Girotti, among others. And as I gather, you manage these three, Signor Scarpa." A half-truth I thought he'd swallow.

"Si, si," he replied, impatience creasing his brow. "Honestly, Ferro, I couldn't care less about this guy's game, whoever he is. How would handwriting samples do any good?"

"In a situation like this," I elucidated with patience, "a private investigator must gather robust evidence. This case may find its way into a courtroom. If I can prove it's not your artists, they're in the clear and won't be disturbed..."

Noticing the gears beginning to turn in his head, I pressed on:

"By aiding me, you're also aiding your clients. All it takes is to unearth some handwriting samples from your archives. It won't take much time."

Scarpa shut his eyes momentarily before reopening them.

"Fine, I suppose there's no harm in it," he conceded wearily. "But I'm not thrilled about it."

He reached for the phone and directed the secretary to bring the files. In under two minutes, the girl entered, her blue hair shimmering, holding a stack of files.

"Here they are, Dottore." With meticulous care, she placed the files on the desk, and he waved her off impatiently.

Flipping open one of the files, I skimmed its contents.

"Hey, those are confidential!" Scarpa protested, attempting to shut the file.

"You promised me samples, Scarpa," I reminded him. "And I need photocopies."

"Are you out of your mind?" He sprang to his feet, surprisingly short in stature. A meaty fist pounded the desk.

I offered no words, maintaining an even gaze on him.

"You've got a couple of days, Ferro," he grumbled. "But I want a report on your findings – if there are any."

"Thanks you, Dottore," I replied and turned to leave.

As I reached the door, his voice called me back.

"Who's your client, Ferro?"

"You, of all people, should understand the necessity of proxies when dealing with clients. I don't ask about your clients, you don't ask about mine. Goodbye."

His stare bore into my retreating back as I closed the door behind me.

At the secretary's desk, I procured the photocopies.

"His acid must be acting up today," she whispered with a wink.

*

Before continuing to Leila Luca's hotel, I made a pit stop at Carlino Transport Company. Nestled in an industrial park near the northern Italian border, their establishment stood as an aged relic amongst several newer, half-completed construction sites. It proved a formidable task to locate anyone acquainted with Scavolini. After considerable effort, I finally cornered a wiry individual sporting a t-shirt adorned with graphics from some rock band's tour.

"Scavolini?" he echoed upon my query. "You're out of luck, Signore. Scavolini isn't here today."

"But he works here, doesn't he?"

"Yeah, he's on my special unit," the man responded. "Name's Tassi. I'm the supposed foreman for this team."

"How long has Scavolini been here?"

He puckered his lips in contemplation. "Let's see... around six months, I reckon. Why do you ask? Who are you?"

"I'm Luigi Ferro, a private investigator," I divulged, flashing my credentials.

He mumbled something and slouched his shoulders. Without a direct glance at me, he muttered, "This is all perfectly legitimate, Signor Ferro. What are you digging after?"

"Just looking into Scavolini."

"Has he stirred up some trouble?"

"I didn't say that."

"So?"

"I believe the Gendarmerie called here earlier today, didn't they?"

"Ah, yes. You're right!" he chimed in as if suddenly recalling. "I didn't take the call; it was young Alfonso. He mentioned it, but I was swamped and didn't think about it. What was it about, truly?" His arms crossed over his chest, and he examined me with a newfound curiosity.

"As I mentioned, I'm keen on learning more about Scavolini. He works as an express courier?"

"Yeah. And he's trustworthy. Has the authorization

to bear arms and engage in tasks others might not be suited for. You know how it goes."

"Indeed," I agreed. "Like transporting valuables? Perhaps cash?"

Tassi erupted into laughter. "Valuable transports? I wouldn't quite phrase it that way. But there are instances when we require an armed guy. We have several assignments involving the transfer of valuable items across the border, and our guys, in a sense, offer security to ensure nothing goes awry... or missing."

"So, Scavolini operates as a sort of armed guard?"

"Well, you wouldn't label him that outright either. You know the situation. Ours is an old-school establishment, Signor Ferro. We're not advertising for heavily armed bodyguards, but opting for a select group of sharp-eyed lads skilled in firearm usage if needed."

"Understood. However, was there an inquiry into Scavolini's background prior to his employment?"

"Presumably," he responded. "I might not be of much assistance on this, Signor Ferro," he added apologetically. "They sent Scavolini my way with the assurance of his reliability and competence. That's pretty much all I've got. For more details, you might be more lucky with the main office."

I regarded him briefly and stated, "I'm just here to talk with someone who has personal knowledge of Scavolini. I doubt I'll get much from the office."

"I see," replied Tassi, contemplatively nodding, though his grasp of the situation was minimal.

"Why hasn't he reported to work today?"

"I'm not certain, Signor Ferro. Maybe he's sick?"

”He didn’t report any reason?”

”No,” Tassi admitted with another shake of his head.

”What does he look like?” I pursued. ”Is he, by any chance, slim, short, dark hair, and…” Thinking of the man who had forced his way into my home last night.

”Oh, no!” Tassi chuckled as if finding my conjecture amusing. ”Scavolini is around one-ninety tall and weighs a solid hundred kilos of muscle.”

”How old is he? About thirty-five?”

”Hmm…” Tassi deliberated, his lips pursed. ”Younger, I’d reckon. Roughly thirty. He’s unmarried, and if memory serves, he resides on the fringes of Rimini. Honestly, Signor Ferro, I’m not well-acquainted with him. He generally keeps to himself.”

”Any places he hangs out?”

”If you’re thinking of bars, you’re out of luck,” Tassi replied, his tone carrying a touch of reproach. ”He abstains from alcohol and tobacco. My understanding is he invests his time at the gym.”

”Any friends around here?”

”I think not. As I mentioned, he’s rather solitary.”

”Very well, thank you,” I acknowledged. ”Your assistance is appreciated.”

”I find that hard to imagine!” he responded earnestly, using one index finger to scratch his head. ”But… would you care to explain… Has Scavolini done something wrong?”

”I’m just gathering information.”

”Can I tell him you were asking about him? Let him know a private investigator has sought him out?”

”Go ahead,” I confirmed. I’d made it partway out the

door before pausing as though suddenly remembering something. "About his firearm," I interjected. "Did he get it from Carlino Transport?"

"His gun? No, that's his personal property."

"Is that normal?"

"No, not exactly. But it must be okay, or Carlino wouldn't have engaged him. Ah, yes, yes, yes!" Tassi exclaimed, tapping his forehead with his knuckles. "I remember now! Scavolini worked for another transport firm before joining us. What was the name...?"

I leaned against the door-frame and waited.

Then, an epiphany struck him. "Ah, got it! Albini & Artoni in Bologna. Maybe they know more about him."

"Perhaps. Many thanks," I acknowledged, departing.

"Absolutely," Tassi affirmed. He reached the door, observing as I zoomed off on my Vespa.

I pulled over at the nearest service station, located the contact details for Albini & Artoni, and dialed the number.

"May I speak to the head of your security department?" I inquired of the lady on the other end of the line.

"The security division?" she echoed.

"Yeah," I confirmed. "The person in charge of armed transports."

"I see," she replied. "Dottore Gerardo. Who may I say is calling?"

"I'm Luigi Ferro," I introduced myself. "A private investigator based in San Marino."

"One moment, please."

I waited for several protracted moments before a deep, resonant voice came through the receiver.

"Pronto. This is Gerardo. What's the matter?"

"Did you employ a guy named Enzo Scavolini about six months ago?" I inquired.

There was a brief pause before he responded, "Scavolini? Yes, certainly. He was among our armed guards responsible for cash transports."

"How long did he work for you, Signor Gerardo?"

"Roughly a year and a half."

"And how did he perform?"

"He…" He paused again before continuing, "Look, I'm not fond of discussing matters like this over the phone."

"I understand your concern, but I'm unable to visit Bologna at the moment."

"How do I know you're legit?"

"You're welcome to verify my license as a private investigator. Additionally, you can contact Comandante Capparoni at the San Marino Gendarmerie."

"Well, your name is familiar, Ferro. I've heard of you," Gerardo acknowledged. "So, I'll take the risk. What's Scavolini involved in now?"

"I'm not entirely certain he's involved in anything," I responded. "What was he doing during his time with your company?"

"We suspect he was part of a bank robbery. If we had solid evidence, he'd be incarcerated by now."

"Ah, I see…" I perked up my attention.

"Scavolini was clever, perhaps a bit too clever for us. He managed to dodge suspicion and navigate quite well for a considerable period. But he wasn't exactly the ideal fit for the role. Then this bank robbery occurred, resulting in two of our guards being shot. While Scavolini was implicated, we couldn't bring charges due to insufficient evidence. Naturally, we dismissed him from our service."

"He likely fabricated a work history from your company to secure a position at Carlino."

"Carlino, you say? They must be complete imbeciles! Although they've always operated on the shadier side of the industry. They never matched our standards."

"Why does he still have a gun license?"

"I didn't know he had one. The weapon he used during his work with us belonged to the company."

"It wasn't a Browning, was it?"

"No, it was a PPK, and it was registered under the company."

"Thank you, that's what I needed for the moment," I acknowledged. "Your assistance is greatly appreciated."

"Don't mention it," Gerardo replied. "If you uncover any developments regarding Scavolini, please do inform me. It'd be satisfying to hear that he's finally met his due... the rat!"

4

I stepped into the vestibule of the timeworn roadside hotel en route to Rimini. A certain mustiness pervaded the air despite the modern chrome accents and scarlet plastic-covered chairs placed haphazardly among pots containing withering palms.

The porter was stationed at his desk.

"Can I help you, Signore?"

"I am Luigi Ferro. I'm seeking one of your guests, Signorina Luca."

"Signorina Luca," he echoed. A hint of hesitation lingered in his expression.

"Is she not in?"

My tone must have conveyed my urgency.

His gaze lingered on me, and he hesitated before responding, "No, Signore, she is not out. However, she's not feeling well."

"Is she sick?"

"Not exactly, Signore. But..."

"Listen," I insisted. "I know Signorina Luca, and I need to see her now."

"I think I must talk to the owner first, Signore."

"Is it that serious?" He again assessed me intently, then picked up the phone receiver and engaged in a hushed conversation.

I leaned against the counter, rhythmically tapping my fingers on its surface.

The porter concluded his exchange. "The owner, Signor Vito, will be here shortly."

"What's wrong with her?" I inquired.

"I can't discuss that with you, Signore."

"If you insist," I acquiesced, turning my attention to a diminutive, somewhat comical-looking man advancing toward me. He was diminutive throughout, donned a tidy ensemble, wore a carnation in his lapel, and sported a bow tie snugly encircling his neck. His visage glistened from aftershave application.

"So, what can I do for you?"

"I'm here to meet Leila Luca," I elucidated.

"Do you know her?"

"Absolutely," I confirmed. "She's my client. I am a private investigator."

He nodded as though my revelation harmonized perfectly with his existing knowledge.

With that, he took hold of my arm, guided me away from the reception desk, and shared in a hushed tone, "Something happened to Signorina Luca last night, however..."

"What happened to her?" I interjected.

Vito swallowed audibly and directed wide-eyed consternation my way. After a moment's pause, he spoke gravely, "She had gone for a stroll for a brief while. Someone attacked her on her way back to her room—between the staircase and her door. The guy hit her on the head. If a maid hadn't come by and scared him off, who knows what would've happened."

"Did anyone see the attacker?" I inquired.

"No, no one saw anything, Signore."

"Did you call the police?"

"Naturally."

"At what time did this happen?"

"Around ten o'clock last night."

"What did the police do?"

"They did a thorough search of the hotel and its surroundings. But the guy was gone–vanished without a trace. We were rather busy last night with a large gathering in the bar. He could easily melt into the crowd and disappear."

"I see," I acknowledged. "How is she doing now?"

"A doctor came, and Signorina Luca has been very lucky. She has a few bruises, but most of all, she is shaken up."

"Makes sense. Anything else you know?" I responded.

"I found out after it happened. Is it possible that someone's got it out for Signorina Luca?"

"Could be," I affirmed, proceeding towards the lodging rooms with Vito trailing behind.

"I wouldn't disturb her now, Signore."

"In that case, you'd better accompany me upstairs and grant me access."

I scaled the staircase in a series of determined strides. Along the corridor's expanse, Vito confided, "Did you know she hails from Puglia?"

"Why?" I inquired.

"Maybe you can persuade her to return home, Signore?"

I regarded him, standing before her chamber door.

"I don't think she's safe here, Signore."

Without further discourse, he inserted a master key

into the lock, turned it, and delivered a gentle rap on the partially open door.

”Who is it?” a faint voice emanated.

Vito leaned in and remarked, ”A surprise for you, Signorina Luca,” infusing a patronizing tone into his words as though addressing a child.

”Oh, Luigi!” she exclaimed as I slipped past Vito.

Leila Luca elevated herself in bed, extending her arms toward me.

My gaze shifted between Vito and her. Then he subtly shook his head, and as he exited, the door shut with a resolute click, leaving us in solitude.

I traversed the room to reach her bedside. She seized me tightly.

”You’ve had an interesting time here,” I mused.

”Luigi,” she uttered between sobs, ”I am so glad to have you here.”

”Stay calm. Everything will soon be alright.”

”And,” she clung to me, ”I was so scared.”

My neck began to ache as I stood, one arm enveloping her trembling form. I had apprised Caterina that Leila possessed an entirely distinct countenance from her elder sister Marilena. Yet, I had neglected to impart that one’s stature need not exceed the average, nor should their body mimic a model’s proportions to be deemed beautiful. In the present moment, Leila Luca, the girl from the hinterlands, bore disheveled hair and a complete absence of makeup. And half of her face, from the browline to the chin, bore the cruel hues of bruises. And she wept.

But even still, she was beautiful.

She projected an aura of fragility and femininity as

she turned toward me, her sobs punctuating the air. The scent of sun and citrus groves wafted from her hair. Tears coursed down her lips, yet she seemed indifferent to their cascade. She clung to me, a profound reliance woven within her touch. At that precise instant, the girl from Puglia outshone her sister in beauty.

After a protracted pause, I gently urged, "Try to relax now."

I delicately lowered her back onto the pillow. She gazed up at me, her lips quivering with emotion.

"Now, if you would, tell me what happened, my dear."

"Look here!" She turned her head slightly, unveiling the discolored contusions.

"Did the doctor give you any treatment?" I inquired.

She offered a subtle nod. "Yeah, some ointment and sleeping pills. I slept, but I still feel awful."

"Yes, I am familiar with the distress it can breed."

"Do you think I'm foolish?" A tinge of blush tinged her cheeks. "You're doing all this for me, aren't you?"

"Don't worry about it. It's my job. Did you see the guy who did this?" I asked.

"Just a quick glance," she replied. "It all happened so fast..."

"Yes, yes," I muttered. "Was he tall or short? Muscular?"

"I'd say tall and quite bulky. He held me with one hand and hit me with the other."

"Did he have gloves on or some type of weapon? The luck that saved you, Leila..."

"I know, Luigi. But knowing that doesn't make me

feel any better..." She shook her head sadly. "Luigi, I'm scared!"

With a measured motion, I extended my hand toward her; it was high time this young woman received some form of consolation. And, perchance, I was in need of solace myself.

She muttered something as my presence drew nearer, though she rapidly overcame her hesitance, wrapping her arms around my neck and pulling me closer still. Her lips, soft yet resolute, met mine in a kiss—gentle yet potent.

It was a kiss, and in its wake...

"Luigi!" she gasped, her words breathless. "Kiss me again, but longer this time!"

*

I pressed Caterina's number on my mobile and awaited her response. The signals continued for an extended moment before the line connected.

"Hello, dear," her voice greeted with a hint of a yawn. "Are you at the office, working?"

"Indeed," I replied, fabricating a half-truth while my gaze inadvertently drifted towards the bed, where Leila rested naked beneath the embrace of a white sheet. Her eyes met mine, a soft smile gracing her lips.

"Perhaps you can be of assistance," I proposed to Caterina. "A friend of mine is in trouble. Can you help?"

"Leila?" Caterina's breath hitched, registering the revelation.

"Yes, precisely."

"Are you with her right now?"

"She got attacked last night," I disclosed. "She needs a safe place to stay. Do you happen to know of anyone trustworthy who could offer her refuge for a few days? As a precaution, of course."

A hush draped over the line.

"She could come here," Caterina offered.

"To you?"

"Why not? I have a guest room that is always vacant. I could also ask Signora Ricci to extend her care."

"It could potentially be hazardous," I cautioned.

"For me? Just bring her here, Luigi."

"At present, Leila Luca could be regarded as a volatile entity."

"Yes, well, I'm sure you're not doing anything to mitigate that volatility," Caterina joked, her sardonic amusement palpable.

I resisted the urge to bite back at her teasing.

"But you do know her sister, correct?"

"Marilena? I'm prepared to take the risk if Leila is okay with it?"

"I don't want her staying any longer in that hotel."

"She could, hypothetically, return to that... well, whatever that village in Puglia was called?"

"Mind your words, my dear," I interjected.

"She's with you, isn't she? Will she be a difficult guest, Luigi? Should I expect weeping and wailing due to her injuries?"

"Not at this time, at least."

"Good, you're focused on her care. I'm crazy about you, you know."

Hearing Caterina's words, I took a deep breath.

”I'll be with you within the hour, accompanied by the young lady.”

”For the love of all that's good, Luigi, can't you end our conversation with a sweet sentiment? Say 'I love you too, Caterina' or something of the sort.”

”Indeed. See you soon, my dear.”

I terminated the call.

Leila scrutinized me earnestly and inquired, ”Does Caterina love you, Luigi?”

I approached her, my voice softening, ”It's time for you to rise from this bed, get dressed, and accompany me to San Marino.”

”She cannot love you as much as I do, Luigi.”

”Is that so?”

”Kiss me again...”

”It's high time you got up.”

”Only after you kiss me again.”

I leaned down, acquiescing to her request, and she pulled me gently beside her.

”Be careful with your shoulder, dear,” I admonished.

”I have other things on my mind,” she murmured, pressing her body against mine.

5

Within the hour, we found ourselves standing before an ancient dwelling on a narrow, cobblestone lane. The house was a century-old edifice, its timeworn bricks and mortar exuding a sense of history that contrasted sharply with the modern world. Ivy clung to the walls, creeping its way toward the weathered shutters. Leila got off the Vespa, her eyes widening as she took in the scene, finally resting on the house's antiquated turret. "Luigi... This place looks old," she murmured.

"Yeah, it's got history. Let's go," I prompted, taking hold of her bag.

She lingered on the pavement, a shadow of apprehension crossing her features. "I'm scared, Luigi. I just want to go home."

"Home's not safe right now. Zegno di Puglia is as secure for you now as Afghanistan is for a woman in a bikini."

She sighed, reluctantly ascending the steps toward the entrance gate. Leila hesitated as we approached Caterina's door, uttering, "What if she doesn't like me?"

"You'll be fine," I assured her, appraising her appearance critically. She was clad in the same unremarkable ensemble she had worn during her initial visit to my office. Makeup concealed the worst of her bruises, applied with assistance from one of the hotel staff. Her lips curved into a somber expression until she noticed my gaze on her. At that point, she brightened, managing a tentative smile.

"That's my girl."

"I wish I was really your girl!"

I knocked on the door, and Leila slipped her arm under mine, her trembling palpable. The door swung open.

"You've made it," Caterina greeted with a sneer.

"We didn't have to fend off any gangsters," I remarked, observing the mutual scrutiny between the two women. Caterina wore a simple dress cinched with a sash at the waist. A vivid red ribbon adorned her dark hair, and her makeup bore the touch of a planned outing.

"I just crawled out of bed," she fibbed, her tone light. "Please forgive my appearance. Since Luigi is too modest to make introductions... my name is Caterina Curiale. Nice to meet you."

"Thanks for having me," Leila responded, sounding dignified and composed. She pulled back her hand from Caterina's grasp and continued, "Luigi said you know what's going on, so..."

"...there's no need for long explanations," Caterina completed, her smile unwavering. "Please, Leila, have a seat. Signora Ricci will be delivering lunch shortly, and in the meantime..."

"A drink, perhaps?" I interjected.

"Let's get Leila settled first," Caterina proposed, gesturing toward the luggage.

I nodded, hoisting the bag.

"Would you care for some coffee?" Caterina inquired of Leila.

"That would be lovely."

"Milk?"

Leila shook her head, trailing me through the apartment. We ascended two steps, bridging the gap between the living area and the sleeping quarters, until we reached the door opposite Caterina's bedroom. I swung the door open and set the bag down.

"It looks cozy," Leila remarked, her gaze sweeping the room.

"Make yourself at home. I'll get Caterina to bring your coffee."

Upon my return to the living room, Caterina seized my arm.

"Don't rush off just yet. Luigi, you're a damn liar!"

I met her gaze, intrigued.

"You said she was plain! But she's sheer elegance... She could be stunning if she knew how to dress and do her makeup. Luigi?"

"Yes?"

"Are you a blind fool, or do you genuinely see her as dull and common?"

"You're talking too much," I shot back.

I wrapped an arm around her, tilted her backward, and planted a kiss on her lips. She responded as if she'd waited that moment for ages, parting her lips to meet mine.

"Don't even think about trying to distract me, Luigi Ferro!"

I kissed her again, then released her.

"You're gonna be the death of me," she warned.

"Thanks for helping out, Caterina," I acknowledged.

"Indeed, I'm feeling like a good Samaritan today," she quipped, playing with the ribbon adorning her hair. Her eyes sparkled at me.

"Luigi... guess who called just now? Marilena!" she exclaimed without waiting for a response.

"So, what?"

"Is that your only reaction? No surprise or even a hint of shock? Honestly, I was taken aback. She called right after you did, and..."

"If that's the case, we need to get Leila out of here quickly!"

"But, Luigi..."

"How much did you tell to Marilena, Caterina? You might be getting yourself in a situation that's..."

"... and you're leaping to conclusions! Take a breath, darling. I handled Marilena just fine. She was so busy talking about herself she didn't even notice anything was up. Guess what? She's engaged to Lawrence Mims."

I poured a glass of wine and regarded her. "Who in the world is Lawrence Mims?"

"Are you completely oblivious to the gossip? Lawrence Mims is Italy's most eligible bachelor. Rich and single. Or was. Regardless, it's a triumph for La Lisa."

"In what way?"

"This was shared with me in strictest confidence!" Even Caterina sounded smug. "Marilena's announcing her engagement on her show tonight. She's invited friends to be in the audience."

"Then, I'll be there to cheer her on."

"You?"

"Yeah. Although she might have overlooked that fact. Last night, she requested to meet up after the show."

Caterina regarded me with a furrowed brow. "You certainly don't waste any time."

"Seems La Lisa is swifter still. This engagement might be why she's pushing her plans."

"Marilena doesn't let anything get in her way. Especially not when it comes to getting married. Speaking of which, her ex Franco Marini won't be happy when he hears the news."

"The singer?"

"Yes! Her second husband, if you remember?"

"Why?"

"He's been sending her flowers recently. Plus, he's returned here trying to get a musical TV show with Umberto Di Mauro."

"Di Mauro?" I feigned astonishment.

"Don't act clueless!" Caterina shot back, her eyes gleaming. "But you're right. Our television emperor also has romantic ambitions."

"For the small screen's reigning beauty, I presume?"

"Clearly, you're out of touch with the media."

"I spend my spare time with books," I shrugged.

"Marilena isn't just the media's darling; she's also a force of nature."

"Let's get back to her younger sister."

Caterina nodded in contemplation. "The younger sister isn't just the countryside girl you take her for, Luigi."

"No?"

"There's more to her than meets the eye."

Caterina went to fetch Leila from her unpacking, and the latter settled down, savoring a hot double espresso. She gazed up at us serenely.

"I hope you'll be comfortable here, Leila," Caterina offered.

"How kind of you."

"And," I interjected, "Caterina will keep strangers away and keep you within these walls. And you'll have to stay here until I come back for you, Leila."

She got up abruptly, causing the dark liquid to almost spill. "Luigi... you're not leaving me here all alone, are you?"

"I have other things to do, Leila. You'll be perfectly fine here."

"Of course," Caterina chimed in with a grin and placed a hand on her arm. "I might be crazy, but I'm harmless. Isn't that right, Luigi?"

"Absolutely," I agreed, playfully ruffling her hair.

"In case you're wondering, Leila," she said in a more earnest tone, "I do the weather on SMTV, but music's my real passion. I've even done some work for independent movies and television and even created the opening theme for Marilena's show."

"I like music," Leila responded solemnly. "When Maria and I were kids, we used to write songs that Maria would sing."

A brief yet awkward silence settled in. But I broke it. "For now, I want you to put aside any thoughts of Maria... Marilena Lisa. And don't worry about anything, sweetheart."

"I'll try, Luigi."

"Now, I must be on my way. Just one more thing – I'd like to have the last letter you received."

She regarded me searchingly. "You mean the anonymous letter?"

I nodded.

"I've got it in my bag."

As she rummaged through her purse, Caterina and I exchanged a meaningful glance.

"You won't receive any more letters like that," I reassured her.

Without a word, she handed me the letter.

"Bet you took some detours getting here, huh? Just to shake off potential followers," Caterina remarked with an effort to sound cheerful.

"We managed to leave everything behind. Isn't that so, Leila?"

"I don't think we were followed," she responded hesitantly.

"You've got no reason to worry about that," I asserted, patting her shoulder. "You're safe here. No letters, no calls, no visitors."

"Except from you, Luigi."

"Yes."

"And maybe..." She hesitated, and I couldn't help but notice her blush. "I have a friend in Bologna. He... he might be worried."

I regarded her closely. "Why haven't you told about him before, young lady? Who is this man?"

"His name is Emilio Pisa. He works for the insurance company Genco and had a lot to do with the city council where I work. Then he moved to Bologna, and well... I met him before I came to you, Luigi."

"Does Pisa know your sister?" I inquired.

She gave a solemn nod. "He knows all about her. He was with me when I first tried to contact her, and she turned me down. We're just close friends, nothing more." Her gaze shifted away swiftly. "Emilio and I are close friends... but nothing more."

"A man can't simply be a close friend and nothing more," Caterina interjected with a trace of sarcasm. An awkward silence followed.

After a while, I spoke up. "So, what's the story with this Pisa fellow?"

"If I could call him at his office? Just to let him know I'm alright?" Leila proposed.

"As long as you don't say where you are. You mustn't reveal that under any circumstances."

"I won't, Luigi," she assured. Then she added, "You can trust Emilio. He's not a member of Marilena's fan club. Which... which sort of puts him on our side, doesn't it?"

I didn't respond directly to her question, but I did say, "Why doesn't he like her?"

"Well... that insurance company, Genco, dealt with Umberto Bortoloni, Maria's first husband. Emilio had to clean up a lot of messes with insurance stuff and Umberto's estate."

"That girl really knows how to complicate life," Caterina remarked.

"I suggest locking the door, Caterina," I advised.

"This place is like Fort Knox; it's been here for

centuries, and it will hold a few days more, darling. Can I venture out and see my friends? Or am I also under house arrest?"

"You might want to cut back on those detective shows," I teased.

I glanced at both of them, concluding that it was best for me to leave the premises.

*

The day was winding down at six in the evening, and the constant flow of tourists had thinned out as I returned to my office at Piazza della Libertà. Finally, a moment of respite to delve into the task at hand: scrutinizing the handwriting samples I'd obtained from Scarpa. Placing the photocopies on my desk, I flicked on the lamp to better illuminate the pages. Carefully, I positioned the anonymous letter given to me by Leila next to the copy of Marilena Lisa's writing.

Starting with one set of samples and then the other, it didn't take an expert to discern the striking resemblance in the styles. An adept forger might write backward to fake his natural, but the person behind the anonymous letters had attempted simpler tactics to mask their handwriting—altering slants, adding twists and flourishes to obscure the original hand. Nevertheless, beneath the bright lamp's glow, the commonality was evident.

Tossing aside the remaining handwriting samples, I tucked the anonymous letter alongside Marilena's examples into an envelope, sealed it with a lick, and stowed it within a desk drawer. As the drawer closed, a knock echoed at my door. While unexpected visits weren't uncommon, I'd grown accustomed to clients appearing at all hours.

"The door's open!" I called out.

The knob turned, and the door swung inward. A man's voice sounded tentative yet confident: "May I come in?"

"Absolutely."

Stepping across the threshold, he gently shut the door behind him.

"Furio Renzetti," he introduced himself with a faint smile.

With his name offered up as though it held intrinsic meaning, he awaited my recognition. I leaned back in my chair, appraising him. A svelte, well-dressed man, likely approaching fifty but radiating a youthful aura. His dark hair bore strands of gray, his olive complexion exuding an air of distinction. The carefully groomed mustache added a touch of refinement.

"I'm Marilena Lisa's attorney," he stated.

"And what brings you to my office?" I inquired.

Seating himself, he chose his words carefully, crossing his legs as he did.

"Thank you." He regarded me calm and composed. "I've just come from Renato Scarpa's office, the artist agency."

"Oh?"

"He spoke to me about a certain arrangement he has with you regarding some of his artists."

"Is that so?"

"Doesn't that raise any concerns for you?"

”Why would it?” I gestured toward the modest confines of my office. ”Please, continue, Signor Renzetti.”

”To be frank, Scarpa revealed your agreement with him, and I felt it was crucial to seek you out immediately.”

”What's the big deal?”

”First, I contemplated calling you,” he said, choosing his words meticulously. ”But I decided an in-person visit might be more fitting.”

”And here I am,” I replied, indicating the modest surroundings of my workspace. ”What can I do for you, Renzetti?”

”Truth be told, the nature of your arrangement with Scarpa has raised some concerns for me,” he said.

Renzetti shrugged nonchalantly, producing a silver cigarette case. He extended it toward me, a silent offer that I declined with a shake of my head, though I gestured that he was welcome to light up. His legs crossed again as he leaned back, taking a few deliberate drags. As he exhaled bluish tendrils of smoke, his gaze fixed on the ceiling as he began to speak.

”Scarpa was deeply troubled by the recent events. He seemed to sense an air of suspicion surrounding the entire situation. Given my role as Marilena Lisa's attorney, he believed it necessary to keep me informed.”

I leaned forward, inquiring, ”And what about Marilena Lisa?”

His stare sharpened, assessing my reaction. ”You seem more interested in her than the other artists Scarpa mentioned.”

”What gives you that impression?”

”Bits and pieces that have come to my attention.”

"Like what?"

"For a start, I learned of your presence at Umberto Di Mauro's gathering last night."

"As were numerous others."

"True, but you were seen engaged in conversation with Signora Lisa. Following that exchange, you departed the event. This didn't go unnoticed and generated some lively discussions."

"In a small community like ours, gossip becomes daily reading," I remarked, thinking that in a state of less than thirty-five thousand, even the slightest gossip became country-wide news.

His lips formed a slight purse. "Don't get me wrong," he stated. "Marilena Lisa is a prominent figure, perpetually under the spotlight. Naturally, as her legal counsel, I notice when someone like you gets close, Signor Ferro."

"Just doing my job."

"Same here," he responded, leaning forward to flick ash off his cigarette. "When Scarpa recounted your visit today, I felt compelled to seek out the underlying truth."

"Scarpa knows the details."

"But not all, Signor Ferro. He mentioned one of your clients being harassed by an unknown individual."

"Unhinged," I lied. "This person has become a significant nuisance to my client. Sending anonymous letters signed by Scarpa's artists, including Marilena. I got handwriting samples to check it out."

"May I take a look at those letters?"

"I'm afraid that's not possible."

"Do you have them here?"

"No, I keep them safe," I replied.

"So, these letters hold substantial value?"

"Let's just say they're hot potatoes."

Our eyes locked in a silent exchange of intent and knowledge. I was eager to gauge the extent of his awareness and discern how much he might be speculating.

Eventually, he broke the silence. "It still appears that your primary interest lies with Marilena Lisa. I'll be frank with you, Signor Ferro. As Marilena Lisa's attorney for many years, I have an understanding of her that few possess."

"Consider yourself fortunate," I quipped.

"Indeed," he agreed, his smile wry. "Fortunate enough to be well-acquainted but not fortunate enough to have her to myself."

His speech echoed with the tone of a schoolboy, yet I sensed authenticity beneath his words.

"Numerous men would love to marry Marilena Lisa," I commented, raising an eyebrow. "So, I'd suggest you join the queue, Renzetti."

He managed a forced chuckle. "That's hardly relevant. I wanted to let you know that Marilena has been quite affected by certain letters she's received."

"Letters?" I feigned surprise.

"To be blunt, they've been blackmail letters, Signor Ferro."

I leaned back in my chair, interlacing my fingers behind my neck as I observed him.

"You don't appear surprised," he remarked. "But it seems you're well-informed about these blackmail attempts."

"Do you think so?"

"Let's not dance around, Signor Ferro. I'm aware that Leila Luca is here in town."

I let my chair slide back to its normal position and rested my hands on the desk. Renzetti extinguished his cigarette, and smoke lazily curled between us, ascending toward the ceiling.

"Very well, enough games," I acquiesced. "What do you really know about Marilena and Leila?"

"I believe I'm well-informed about everything," he replied coolly. "It's part and parcel of my profession."

"As Marilena's legal representative, you're likely aware that she's refused any contact with Leila and distanced herself from her?"

"It's a possibility."

"And do you have an opinion on that matter?"

"I am not expected to take sides in such affairs, Signor Ferro. It's Marilena's prerogative to decide whether she wants to engage with Leila or not. Marilena is currently at the zenith of her career. Why would she permit past issues to hinder her success?"

"You sound like her PR guy, Renzetti," I remarked.

He blushed slightly, his expression growing a tad more resolute. "That may be the case. Nevertheless, I maintain that Marilena retains her right to make her own choices."

"She's free to assert that she believes Leila is behind these threats, correct?"

Renzetti locked his gaze onto me, and after a contemplative moment, he nodded slowly.

"So, Leila is your client?"

"Aren't you getting ahead of yourself, Renzetti?"

"I don't believe I am." He rose from his seat, coming to stand at my desk, his posture taut and unyielding.

"Your visit to Scarpa's today was merely a trial run, wasn't it? You were seeking a sample of Marilena's handwriting to compare it with..." He hesitated before continuing, "...certain letters you have in your possession."

I met his gaze without an immediate response.

"Don't try to manipulate me," he snapped. "I'm not naive, Signor Ferro. Marilena received blackmail letters, whereas Leila received anonymous threats. And there have been attempts on her life. What have you got to say about that, Signor Ferro?"

"Even if I knew anything, I'd leave it to the court to decide, Renzetti."

He stood rigid for a moment before bursting into laughter. "You're bluffing!"

I joined the laughter, replying, "Bluffing isn't necessary. I'm just doing my job. I'll find out who's behind all this and take it to the district attorney."

A slight twitch tugged at the corner of his mouth.

"You wouldn't dare push it that far," he asserted.

"He who lives shall see," I retorted.

We held each other's gaze in a prolonged silence.

"Listen, Ferro," he began, his tone more measured. "I represent Marilena Lisa, a figure of far greater significance than Leila Luca could ever hope to be. Let me make this clear: If you bring legal action, we'll hit back hard."

With that, he spun on his heels and headed for the door.

Just as his hand reached the doorknob, I interjected, "Are you coming to the studio tonight? For her show?"

He halted, a perplexed look crossing his features. "Studio? What are you talking about?"

I shrugged nonchalantly. "So, you haven't been invited? Word is, she's set to announce her engagement tonight."

He took a tentative step toward me, his face suddenly blanching.

"Engagement?" he managed, his voice strained.

"Well, I'm simply passing on what I've heard," I replied with an unconcerned gesture.

Reclining in my chair, I observed the growing nervousness emanating from him.

"Who's she planning to marry?" Renzetti snapped abruptly.

I raised a hand in a casual gesture. "I believe his name is Lawrence Mims."

A pause hung between us.

"Ah, yes, of course," he stuttered, attempting to regain his composure. "Mims, of course."

"Rich guy, huh?"

"Wealthy and accomplished," Renzetti affirmed. "And evidently, a fortunate man. I thought he'd given up hope."

"See you at the studio tonight, Renzetti," I remarked, feigning indifference.

"Perhaps," he muttered before extending his hand abruptly. "My apologies if I was a touch brusque earlier. Truth be told, I've been quite concerned for Marilena lately."

"I can understand that," I responded as I released his hand. "But with Lawrence Mims, she probably won't have to worry about blackmail, right?"

He shrugged uncertainly.

"You might be onto something. Yet, what's the point?" He forced a smile. "Clients can be an absolute enigma at times, Signor Ferro. The successful ones, particularly. Good evening."

"See ya," I bid him farewell as he closed the door behind him.

Sinking back into my chair, I stared at the door, pondering the exchange. Blackmail and threats, attempts on my client's life, and a lawyer who seemed to have more interest than business in his client.

A shrill ring from the telephone brought me back to reality. I reached for the device, noticing the call was from an unknown number.

"Pronto! Luigi Ferro speaking."

"Hello," a soft and veiled voice greeted me.

Initially, I struggled to place the voice. "Don't you recognize my voice, Luigi? Do I sound that different from TV? It's Marilena Lisa."

"Ah, yes, of course," I responded. "How are things on your end?"

"You may have forgotten, but I promised to meet you after tonight's show."

"And now you're calling to cancel?"

"Oh, no! But would it be possible to meet me before I head to the studio?"

"Where are you now?"

"At home, in my house."

”Sounds good.”

”Come over, have a drink, and let's chat.”

”Sounds like a plan.”

She provided her address and added, ”You're among the first to hear the shocking news. I'm about to tie the knot, Luigi!”

”Congratulations.”

”Thank you. I'm over the moon. Made up my mind this morning. Lawrence Mims is the lucky man. You're not familiar with him, I assume?”

”I've come across the name,” I admitted.

”Excellent. See you shortly, Luigi.”

”See you soon.”

I hung up the phone. Was this good news? Our confident talk was expedited, and Marilena Lisa sounded relieved, if not happy?

*

I dialed Petrelli's number at the Gendarmerie. He picked up, his voice brimming with cheerfulness and confidence.

”Scavolini? No, we haven't managed to nab him yet, Ferro. It's like he's vanished into thin air.”

”Just wanted to touch base,” I replied.

”Good timing,” Petrelli continued. ”I've got some news for you from our fingerprint experts regarding those faint prints you snapped on the Browning.”

”And?”

”They've ID'd two sets of prints. An unknown woman's and those of a known criminal, Abdiel.”

”Abdiel?”

"Yes, he's on our list."

He paused for a moment, then added, "His full name is Enzo Abdiel. His mother's name was Mary Scavolini."

"Scavolini? Looks like we hit the jackpot."

"You could say that. Abdiel did a five-year stint for drug trafficking and possession of unlicensed firearms. Records indicate he was affiliated with Bardo's mafia-like syndicate for a while before he vanished."

"So he's resurfaced," I mused. "If this is the same guy, Scavolini has been working as an armed guard for a couple of respectable transport companies in the past couple of years."

I shared the details of my ongoing investigation with Petrelli. Once I'd finished, he said, "We're going to give him what he deserves. If Enzo Scavolini is indeed Enzo Abdiel and the one who shot at you."

"Then let's just keep him on ice," I suggested.

"More like fiery ice," Petrelli chuckled. "Stay tuned."

We ended the call simultaneously.

I n the marble foyer of the house that felt less like a home and more like a glossy tableau in a luxury lifestyle magazine, a maid attired in crisp black welcomed me. Her uniform stood in stark contrast to the setting, which, while meticulously arranged, betrayed a certain sterility. A house that seemed conceived more for the aesthetics than the comfort of its inhabitants.

She led me into what might be termed a 'salon'—the vocabulary seemed to inflate with the price of the real estate. Marilena Lisa sailed toward me over a plush carpet with a confident grace.

"How delightful you could make it," she cooed, extending a hand in welcome. I shook it briefly, noting the chill.

Calling for refreshments with an elegant wave of her hand, she gestured for me to sit. I obliged.

She positioned herself beside an art piece whose meaning eluded me and crossed her arms over her chest. Her face was adorned with an inscrutable smile. Silence settled over us until the maid returned with our drinks, placing them on the table before vanishing as silently as she'd arrived.

"Something other than your usual water?" I inquired.

"Free of alcohol," she confirmed, handing me a glass of gin and lime. "But flavored for those who care for more than just hydration."

"Your memory serves you well," I smiled.

"If you say so, Luigi," she returned my nod and took a sip.

I nodded at her and brought the glass to my lips. First, I noticed the crispness of the gin, infused with herbs, citrus, and floral elements. Followed by the burst of lime, offering a tangy and slightly tart sensation that cuts through the gin's richness.

"Seen my sister again?" she questioned.

"I have," I replied cautiously.

"And?"

"I thought we weren't talking about that," I hedged.

"Oh, we are," she insisted, lowering herself onto a designer chair. "I'm getting married, Luigi. Time to move on. For the first time, the ground beneath my feet feels solid."

"And you think that'll stop the blackmailer?"

"Undoubtedly," she declared. "The leech will find no more blood to draw."

"I think you're wrong," I retorted. "You're marrying a wealthy man; your blackmailer will only increase their demands."

"She hasn't gotten a cent from me. Nor will she ever. You see, it's my sister doing this."

"A claim both foolish and dangerous," I fired back.

"Leila threatens to expose my past to Lawrence Mims," she asserted.

"She wouldn't."

"She did. In her own handwriting."

"And you're convinced your sister believes you've played a part in your first husband's death?"

Marilena erupted from her seat. "How dare you!"

"Spare me the theatrics," I said, cool as ice, even as she hurled her drink in my face.

Slowly rising, I wiped my face with a handkerchief, deliberately folded it, and returned it to my pocket. Taking her by the arms, I gently slapped her on both cheeks, careful not to leave a mark.

"Understand this," I articulated, staring into her incensed eyes, "if you're facing threats, your sister isn't your enemy. But if you continue to slander her, you will find an enemy in me."

"Ah," she sneered, "the loyal guardian."

"Indeed," I affirmed, "Leila is my client. And you should leave her alone."

Marilena stared at me, but I had already made my point. Whatever she chose to believe, whatever course she embarked upon, she had been duly warned.

Marilena's laughter reverberated through the opulent chamber. "She must pay you quite handsomely from her humble civil servant's salary."

"If you had bothered to lend her assistance over the years," I retorted, "her financial circumstances would be different. But generosity was never your strong suit, was it? You're all about you, aren't you? Marrying this Mims is just your next move for a lifetime meal ticket."

As she attempted to rise, I firmly guided her back to her seat.

She fought hard to overcome the humiliation.

"I'll scream and have you arrested," she hissed.

"No," I said, holding her gaze, "you'll sit and listen. Mess with Leila again, and you can forget about marrying Lawrence Mims."

She froze, her eyes losing their fire. "What did you say?"

"Laying it bare, then," I continued, measured. "You've been messing with your sister, even hired a guy to take her out. I've connected the dots. Is that why you tried to have me killed? Is getting engaged to Mims your way out? A desperate act to resolve your little problem?"

"Pour me a drink," she whispered.

I handed her the glass of gin. "It may contain alcohol," I grinned.

"Enough!" She downed it, shattering the glass against the hardwood floor.

She rose, and for a moment, her eyes flamed anew, then dimmed as she slumped into my arms. "You might be a jerk, Luigi, but you're the kind of man I've always fantasized about."

"Will you leave Leila be?" I asked.

"All right," she sighed. "But one condition—a single kiss."

My gaze settled on her. She was physically magnificent, every inch the epitome of femininity and allure. Yet her soul was a festering wound.

"I'm waiting," her voice dropped to a sultry murmur.

Surrendering to the inevitable, I kissed her. Her lips were as toxic as they were inviting, her nails digging into the nape of my neck, her kiss a complex melody of desire and deceit.

An inebriated voice erupted behind us. "Am I interrupting something?"

We disengaged. Marilena turned her attention to a

mirrored compact, freshening her makeup as if nothing had happened.

I sized up the newcomer—a large man with a jester's grin, hands buried in his pockets as he took tentative steps toward me. A face vaguely familiar yet unplaceable.

"Who are you?" I asked, an undercurrent of caution lacing my voice.

Marilena glided to my side, an epitome of grace under duress. "Let me present you two? Luigi Ferro, meet Franco Marini."

"The ex-lover of the woman you just kissed," Marini retorted. He evinced no intention of offering the civility of a handshake. He grinned like a Cheshire cat, a robust figure, clean of jaw and broad of girth. Gradually, the image of his face appeared in my memory, from billboards and vinyl covers from social gatherings of yesteryears. Marini had tasted the ambrosia of fame and languished in oblivion before clawing back to some semblance of relevance.

Marilena interjected, "Let's not make a big deal out of this."

"A drink would be good," I said.

"Ah, the man can talk," Marini sneered, leaning in close. The idiocy of his smile now vanished. "I've heard of you, Luigi Ferro. Think you're some kind of genius sleuth?"

"I've got a license," I returned the smile, though laced with a hint of menace.

"And to what end?"

"To legally deal with idiots who annoy me," I retorted.

Marilena quickly intervened, wedging herself in the

tension-charged air between us. "Franco, having a key to my place doesn't mean you can trash-talk my friends."

Her grip on his arm was a vise, but he shrugged it off vehemently. "Let me go, woman!" Then, snarling at me, he spat, "What's this guy doing with you?"

"For heaven's sake, Franco!" Marilena beseeched. "You're drunk!"

"Being drunk is my business, just like it's my business if I don't like you hanging out with losers."

The retort I chose was of a physical nature—a succinct, biting jab aimed at his ear. He spluttered, stumbled backward, collided with an unfortunate chair, and plummeted face-first onto the floor.

Marilena's laughter was a bright chime in the air. "Once more, Luigi! Do it again!"

"I'll take that drink now," I requested.

As she approached, her sapphire eyes twinkling like stars, she whispered, "Luigi, I could easily forgive that kiss."

She sauntered to the remote bar, returning with a crystal glass of gin. By this time, Marini had regained his footing, and his approach was decidedly less stable. He lurched toward the bar, ignoring me, seized a bottle of whiskey, and guzzled a glass in a singular, desperate swallow. Then, arms swaying, he took uncertain steps in my direction.

"The show's over, Marini," I intoned, eyes locked onto his.

"You think I'm some kind of bad guy, I presume?" he growled.

"I don't waste time thinking about guys like you," I rejoined.

"Rude and disrespectful! Marilena, call the police!" Marini howled.

"Don't be stupid, Franco!"

"Who does this guy think he is? Coming in here, kissing you, hitting me—what a jerk!"

"Want to go another round, Marini?" I closed the distance in a stride, gripping the fabric of his shirt, and landed another punch.

His body teetered on the edge of falling, but I steadied him, my words hissing through clenched teeth.

"Say one more stupid thing, and you won't even recognize yourself."

Peals of laughter erupted from Marilena behind me, and I released my human tether. He tottered back to the bar, where he found solace in another gulp of liquid courage.

"You see the sort of creature I've been dealing with," Marilena sighed.

"That chapter is over," I remarked.

"Indubitably!" she trilled. " I let him on my show, my team made him sound good, and he even cut an album. But then he just messed it all up. And now look at him..."

Her words terminated abruptly, her face a tableau of sudden terror. "Franco, no!"

I hurled myself to the floor; my eyes caught the glint of metal in his trembling hand. The firearm delineated erratic arcs in the air, but it was no illusion.

The glass in my hand became an impromptu projectile, hurled just as his finger squeezed the trigger. The bullet missed its mark, but the glass struck true. I pounced upon him, wrenching the weapon from his grasp after a fierce struggle. It skittered across the carpet, coming to rest against the sofa's leg.

Marini was surprisingly tenacious, landing solid blows. He seemed to be gathering sobriety from the melee. In close quarters, we exchanged punches until an opening allowed me to strike him just below the heart. His body crashed to the floor, bereft of any attempt to cushion the fall.

"I didn't know he had a gun," Marilena gasped.

"Now you do," I said. "But he can't stay here."

"We're pretty isolated here; our neighbors are distant," she noted.

"Your staff?"

"They won't talk," she insisted, administering a contemptuous kick to the fallen Marini, who groaned in response.

"Still, we should get him out of here. Guess you don't need the sordid headlines," I cautioned.

"I can handle Franco," she assured me. "Let's say I have friends."

Pausing at the threshold, I turned back. "Who exactly are these 'friends' you mention, Marilena?"

"It doesn't matter," she said sharply. "Tomorrow is my day, Luigi Ferro. I have told Lawrence Mims everything. The blackmail will no longer be effective."

I departed the sultry outdoor air feeling like an elixir compared to the chill atmosphere I left behind.

7

Slipping into the sumptuous cavern of the Grand Hotel, I found a quiet corner where I could recharge my phone—which had inconveniently perished during my stay with Marilena—and grab something to satiate my hunger. When the damn thing finally resurrected, it protested with a series of insistent vibrations, informing me of several missed calls.

First on the callback list was Caterina. She picked up the phone with a voice choked by raw emotion.

"Luigi! Finally, you've returned my call."

"Spit it out, Caterina. What's wrong?"

"Leila has vanished!"

"What are you talking about?"

"It's the truth, Luigi! She left when I wasn't looking. Had I spotted her, I would have stopped her. But she slinked away the moment I turned..."

"Time. How long ago did she disappear?" I interrupted.

"I can't be certain," she practically wailed. "An hour, perhaps? Your phone was off."

"I was busy. How was she after I left?"

"Normal. Watching TV, listening to me play some songs. It was entirely unremarkable."

"Any phone calls?"

"She called Emilio Pisa, that male acquaintance of hers. You said it was okay."

"Yes, yes," I snapped, my patience waning. "Think she went to meet him?"

"Maybe," conceded Caterina, her voice tinged with apprehension. "But she should've said something. Don't you agree? A *goodbye* would've been courteous."

"Agreed," I muttered. "Was she upset when she spoke to Pisa?"

"No, but it was a long call."

"You left her alone?"

"Yes, Luigi. I was gone for like a half hour."

"Probably when she took off," I surmised. "And Signora Ricci didn't notice?"

"She was in the kitchen, didn't hear a thing. I'm so sorry, Luigi."

"Let's not overstate it. Leila's not a hostage; she's an adult. Maybe she just wanted to go out."

"You don't sound convinced," Caterina quivered. "I feel wretched. Her safety could be in danger, even in the company of this Emilio Pisa. What power does he possess?"

"Your guess is as good as mine," I retorted. "Now, stay put. I'm heading to the TV studio."

"Can't wait to see Di Mauro and Renzetti's faces when they hear about Marilena's engagement," she mused.

"Renzetti already knows. He made a house call to my office today."

"Wow, what a day for you, my dear."

"You have no idea. I also visited Marilena," I said, checking my wristwatch. "Franco Marini showed up and flexed his muscles. But that's a story for another time. I gotta go. And don't do anything stupid without asking me first, Caterina."

"Ha! Like you're mister Careful. Take care, Luigi."

And with that, I disconnected, leaving behind a mountain of unanswered questions and unsettling concerns. What were the reasons behind Marilena's menacing behavior towards Leila? Furthermore, what motivated Leila Luca, the very sister in question, to resort to blackmail against her own flesh and blood? It was a conundrum that seemed out of place, especially considering that she had once found solace in the serene surroundings of Puglia, leading a life that, to any onlooker, appeared to be nothing short of satisfactory.

*

Nestled in the petite enclave of San Marino, proximity is a given. The Television Studio, a hub of fevered activity, shared a sprawling structure with the local Gendarmerie and a theatre. Quite the triumvirate. All were mere strides away from the regal Grand Hotel.

Stepping into the lair of San Marino TV felt like an abrupt shift –from the serenity of a sylvan landscape to a frenzied hive of activity. Down the narrow corridor, a partially ajar door caught my eye. A woman who looked like she might be in charge greeted me.

"Ah, welcome," she sang. "Nibbles and drinks await you inside."

I ambled into the studio, nearly desolate but for a lone woman stationed at the end of a row of seats. Her eyes locked onto mine as she gracefully rose.

"Here for Signor Di Mauro, are you?" she inquired.

"Actually, I'm here for Marilena Lisa," I clarified.

She paused, momentarily struck mute, it seemed. Observing her closely, I could see the signs of a fading beauty. Her ink-black hair had mellowed to a charcoal hue, and her neck had succumbed to the relentless march of time.

"Did I say something wrong?" she finally managed, and I noted a twang of southern Italian accent.

"No, you're good," I said, fetching two goblets from a table against the wall and offering her one.

"How gracious!" She sipped the chilled wine.

"Do you work here?"

"No, no. I am Joana Serra, secretary to Furio Renzetti."

"Ah, the lawyer. We've crossed paths," I said. "Would you like to sit?"

"I'm good standing. I sit all day at work, you see," she replied, taking another sip. Her hand wavered slightly, tipping me off to her concealed nerves.

"So, who are you?" She offered a practiced grin.

"Luigi Ferro, private investigator."

She choked, sputtering wine before turning aside to cough.

"Perhaps a lighter beverage?" I laughed.

"So, you're not here for work?"

"No, it's my night away from the grind," I smiled.

"Do you know Signora Lisa?"

"A bit," I returned.

Just then, a towering figure breezed into the room, a paragon of calculated charm—Umberto Di Mauro on his home turf.

"Ah, Luigi Ferro in the flesh," he declared, a smile revealing a set of immaculate teeth, extending a hand in welcome. "Welcome to SMTV."

He gripped my hand firmly. "Here to catch a star's final local act?"

"Perhaps," I conceded.

Di Mauro glanced at Signorina Serra. "Waiting for someone?"

"Please, don't let me interrupt. I'm but a moth from Renzetti's flame," she stammered.

"Ah, Renzetti is lurking somewhere. Keeping him company?"

"Indirectly. I'm a wallflower, it seems."

"Well then, make yourself comfortable," Di Mauro said, gently patting her shoulder. "As for you, Ferro, shall we?"

I nodded, departing with a backward glance at Serra, whose smile carried a weight of untold concern. Her voice trailed after me.

"Signor Ferro, can I talk to you for a sec?"

Di Mauro was disappearing through a door crowned by a green luminescent bulb. "I'll be right there!" I called out.

He waved dismissively, and I returned to Serra. She nervously clutched her oversized purse against her flat chest as if it could ward off impending doom.

"Signor Ferro, Franco Marini is here and acting weird. He mentioned some news. Do you know if Marilena Lisa is announcing something tonight?"

"It's not a secret anymore," I said, watching her lips quiver.

"He seemed off. Drunk, perhaps," she murmured.

"What did he say?" I pressed.

”That Marilena Lisa might be engaged to be married. Is that true?”

”Could be,” I shrugged, allowing the word to linger in the air, weighted with ambiguity.

Her voice tinged with a poignant earnestness, she queried, ”Is she marrying Renzetti?”

” Why don't you ask him, Signorina Serra? You seem to care a lot about Renzetti,” I noted.

”Years of loyalty,” she whispered as if unveiling a sacred secret.

”So, you want him to get hitched, especially since his business isn't doing so hot?”

”That was rude, Signor Ferro!”

”Why so?”

”Renzetti's had some bad luck in the stock market, but he's still respected, especially in legal circles,” she insisted, her voice quivering as she clutched her oversized purse.

”Very well,” I relented. ”None of my business. Neither is Marilena's,” I added with a playful wink.

”I won't get to talk to her before her announcement,” she said, sounding disappointed.

”At least you're here to witness her final act before she transitions to Rome and the national stage. By local standards, that's quite something,” I said before bidding her farewell.

I hadn't ventured far down the corridor when a voice spoke, ”Please, Signor Pisa, take your seat. The show is about to start.”

”Si, si, grazie,” replied a voice unfamiliar to me.

I kept my gaze forward, pacing toward the door

adorned with a green light. Just before crossing the threshold, I quickly looked down the corridor. A tall, athletically built young man was in conversation with the hostess. "You must be Emilio Pisa?" I probed.

He sized me up, suspicion clouding his eyes. "Si, Signore."

"Luigi Ferro," I introduced myself.

The revelation hit him like a bolt of lightning, a palpable shock registering on his face. He seemed to contemplate making a dash for it. I seized his arm.

"Ferro," he hissed.

"Where is she?"

"What are you talking about?"

"We need to talk. Somewhere private," I suggested.

Tightly gripping his arm, I guided him into another studio. It was dimly lit, too dim to clearly reveal his facial features. Yet, I sensed his mood darken.

"Spill it. What do you know about Leila Luca?" I demanded.

"She's here, and she's safe," he said, a hint of composure returning.

"Did you make her leave Caterina's place?"

"Not exactly," he muttered, his voice tinged with reluctance.

I gripped him firmer, my patience waning. "Listen, Pisa, this is serious. Lying now will make things worse for you—and Leila."

"Va bene," he conceded. "But there's no need to get rough."

The room remained shrouded in murk, but the atmosphere was charged with a different kind of darkness. One that both of us sensed but neither was willing to articulate—yet. Pisa seemed to grapple with the gravity of the situation, the weight of his words settling around us.

"All right. What happened?" I asked, keeping my eyes locked on his.

"Leila called me, and we spoke about you," he said, his voice steadier than before. "We're both grateful to you, Ferro, but—"

"Skip the pleasantries," I interrupted. "You got a call."

"Yes," he continued, "Leila called, and later I called her back. I thought I was being followed by a guy named Scavolini."

"Enzo Scavolini!" My eyes narrowed at the name, recalling the dubious favors he'd done for Lisa.

Pisa nodded. "I saw him shadowing me. I assumed he was still on Marilena's payroll and shifted his focus from Leila to me when she went off the radar."

"Logical," I said. "Did you mention this to Leila?"

"I did," Pisa confirmed, "but never expected her to freak out about it. She was almost hysterical. We agreed to meet in Ausa Dogana Park. She wanted to confront Marilena."

"And Scavolini?"

"Thought I'd lost him. Not sure, though."

"What's the plan now?" I pressed, shifting my weight from one foot to another.

"I join Leila and stick with her. She's in the audience tonight."

"Then go. Now. Stay with her, and don't let her out of your sight. Capito?"

"Si, Ferro," Pisa said, eyes locked onto mine. "But do you still think Leila's blackmailing her sister?"

"You're well-informed," I said. "For the record, I don't think Leila's guilty. And I've dealt with Marilena. She won't be a problem."

"What does that mean?" Pisa asked, bewildered.

" It means focus on Leila. Keep her safe. That's what matters now," I said, making my way toward the control room.

Pisa followed me. "I know what I have to do," he said a little defensively.

"Then go and do it," I responded, fixing him with a stern gaze.

For a moment, our eyes met, and some unspoken understanding passed between us. Then he turned and strode off in the direction of the audience, his figure disappearing into the blend of shadows and light.

As for me, I walked into the control room, aware that the night was still young and many pieces of the puzzle remained unsolved. But one thing was clear: we were all in a complex web of events, and the strands were pulling tighter. Seated before the array of monitors, I felt a disquieting hum in the recesses of my mind, a nagging suspicion that refused to be silenced. It was as if some elusive clue had flitted across the screen, a shadowy hint that could unravel the tangled web of this familial discord that had turned so virulent. Yet, for all my scrutiny, the screens offered no revelations. I was left in a state of uneasy anticipation, waiting for the next piece of the puzzle to reveal itself.

*

In the nerve center of the bustling control room, an eclectic ensemble of people had gathered. Umberto Di Mauro, exuding an air of unobtrusive authority, sat adjacent to the producer who was orchestrating this televised ballet. Engineers, each a savant in video, sound, or lighting, flanked them like knights in modern armor.

On the other side of soundproof glass, Marilena Lisa was in her element, weaving verbal tapestries with her inaugural guest. Rumor had it he'd been a linchpin in the show's pilot episode and now had come full circle.

To my immediate left, Furio Renzetti was pitched forward in his seat as though any moment might contain a revelation. Joana Serra, his unwavering secretary, endeavored to achieve chameleon-like invisibility against the backdrop of the wall.

Franco Marini was sprawled in an armchair, his disinterest radiating from him like an obnoxious perfume. Alongside him, Renato Scarpa, the managerial impresario, was accompanied by a blue-haired attendant who seemed more nursemaid than office aide. Her purpose, no doubt, was to ensure Scarpa's immediate access to digestive relief in the form of Alka-Seltzer.

Scarpa's rear was home to two mysterious entities. One of whom I identified as Sonia Masco, Marilena's PR oracle. A statuesque figure, she oscillated her foot as though concocting some audacious media gambit in her mind.

Pinned against the wall, like a rare butterfly in a collector's cabinet, was Silvano Ghia, an old comrade of mine. He'd cryptically hinted at an extra layer of drama to tonight's show. Ghia was the lone representative of the press, sniffing around as though a juicy morsel awaited his discovery.

Lawrence Mims, a study in sartorial elegance, commanded the foremost row of the studio audience. He donned a double-breasted jacket of azure hue and sat with a self-assured grin that made him seem privy to secrets that eluded the rest of us. His presence had generated an electric undercurrent of whispered speculation within the room, yet no elucidation was forthcoming.

Marilena Lisa drew her first interview to a close with the deft touch and calculated charm that had catapulted her into the limelight. With a commercial break offering a brief respite, the next sacrificial guest was hastily readied.

Marilena gravitated towards Mims, and he rose to greet her. Their words remained a secret communion as some obliging engineer had silenced her microphone.

Through the obscuring windowpane, I observed Marilena confer with the man who was rumored to soon be her spouse. She meandered over to a side table, pausing to decant water from a carafe into a glass. With measured sips, she seemed to recalibrate her vocal cords.

Her gaze, upon her return to the stage, fleetingly swept over our concealed congregation. But her view, I presumed, offered her nothing more than a smudge of indistinct features. Yet, she beamed into the glaring spotlight.

A discreet tap on my shoulder seized my attention. Emilio Pisa materialized beside me.

I hastily sprang from my perch, making for the exit, Pisa leading the charge.

"Shut the door!" came a frenetic command.

The soundproof barrier clicked shut behind me.

"Scavolini is here," Pisa blurted, voice tinged with both awe and apprehension.

"Where?"

"In the audience."

And so the evening's drama thickened a shade darker.

Plunging myself down the labyrinthine corridor, Pisa's voice rang out from the depths behind me, "Nay, this direction!" Heeding his call, I veered sharply, tailing him as he navigated through a set of solid double doors into a diminutive office, culminating at a fire door.

"The studio doors are locked from the inside," Pisa said, his breath uneven. "This is the only way in."

Sliding my hand beneath the fabric of my jacket, I clasped the cold steel of my gun before proceeding in his wake. We breached the studio's periphery.

"Where is he?" I interrogated, sealing the door behind us.

"At the rear."

"And what of Leila?"

"Seated in the frontmost row, I reckon he's watching her, biding his time."

An avalanche of applause erupted as if on cue, accompanying Marilena's introduction of her distinguished guests, the Capitani reggenti, the two heads of state. My eyes scoured the front row, ultimately settling on the familiar silhouette of Leila's head. Marilena Lisa was in top form tonight, utterly eclipsing even her esteemed invitees.

Suddenly, Pisa tugged at my sleeve, directing my

attention toward the gloomy visage of Enzo Scavolini. Propped against the back wall, he was unmistakably clad in the same coat he wore the night he audaciously opened fire in my residence. His hat was jauntily skewed, and the dim luminescence rendered his countenance sinister.

”Go to Leila,” I commanded Pisa.

”But—”

”Go, now!”

He pivoted and limped hastily toward the front row. I, meanwhile, skulked along the side wall, progressing toward Scavolini with cat-like stealth. When I’d shrunk the distance to a mere three meters, our eyes locked.

”We are pleased to confer upon you the Order of San Marino,” proclaimed one of the Capitani reggenti, met with a chorus of cheers from the audience.

Scavolini’s lips contorted into a sneer as his hand extracted a weapon from his pocket. Lunging forward, the .38 clenched in my grip, I fired. The bullet met its mark, embedding in his right shoulder and sending him sprawling against the wall. The firearm clattered from his grasp; he emitted a stifled gasp. A barrage of rapid, unyielding blows followed, forcing him to his knees before he ultimately crumpled to the floor.

A distant shout reverberated from the room’s forefront. Snatching up Scavolini’s forsaken weapon, I pocketed it and reoriented my focus stage-ward. Marilena Lisa had frozen mid-interview, her posture impeccable even in this surreal moment. She clutched the case containing the Order of Merit, its white cross brilliantly illuminated. She maintained her regal stance for several seconds, but then her visage blanched, contorted by an inexplicable agony.

She collapsed forward, her face tinged with surprise and pain, in total silence. Her frame quivered momentarily but ceased almost instantaneously. And so she lay, a tragic still life amidst chaos.

8

Amid the piercing screams from a woman in one of the front rows, the audience had been jolted to their feet. Emilio Pisa navigated his way through the crowd, a look of worry etched on his face. Following close behind him, Leila Luca appeared.

"Luigi, what's going on? What happened to Marilena?"

I yanked Scavolini's gun from my pocket and thrust it into Pisa's unsteady hands. "Keep an eye on Scavolini," I commanded. "Leila, stay with him."

As I turned to leave, Pisa's voice stopped me, tinged with tension. "What about the audience?"

"No one leaves until the police get here," I replied firmly.

I exited the studio, securing the soundproof doors behind me. Midway down the shadowy corridor, a man burst from another door, almost colliding with me.

"Whoa," I cautioned. "You from the studio?"

"Signore!" he cried out, shaking. "Marilena Lisa is dead!"

"Go back," I ordered. "Don't let anyone touch her. Understand?"

"Are you a cop?" he stammered.

"Yes," I lied to save me a lengthy explanation, watching him dash back into the studio. Disquieted murmurs filled the air, but my focus shifted toward the offices.

Inside, the staff buzzed with a mixture of confusion

and dread. "I heard a shot," one receptionist was saying. "Inside the studio."

Brushing past the reception, I made my way to the tranquil courtyard and dialed. As I waited for the call to connect, Umberto Di Mauro emerged from the building.

"Is Comandante Capparoni there? This is Luigi Ferro," I spoke into the phone.

Di Mauro hurriedly approached. "Ferro, you're here?"

I waved him off, palm over my phone's microphone. "Quiet, I'm on the phone?"

"The police—"

"I'm talking to them. Get your staff to the studio. No one leaves. Got it?"

He nodded, though a frantic look still clouded his eyes. "Ferro... she's dead. Marilena Lisa—"

I raised my hand to silence him. "Capparoni, it's Ferro. I need a patrol at SMTV Studios. Marilena Lisa is dead. It may be murder."

"Murder?" Umberto Di Mauro's voice cracked, standing there beside me.

My hand once again shielded the microphone from any ambient noise. "Di Mauro, do you want justice or not?"

"The murderer!" He spat the word out like a vile taste. "So she was actually murdered?"

"You're quick on the uptake," I retorted. "Now go lock the place down until the police get here, will you?"

Moving as if entranced, Di Mauro turned to seize one of the restless guards hovering in the vicinity. His hands shaped the air as he began barking commands. I withdrew my hand from the microphone.

"The asylum's open for business," I said, allowing a note of disdain to color my voice as I spoke to Capparoni. "That was Di Mauro, the SMTV director. You know him?"

"A patrol has already been dispatched," Capparoni intoned, ever the picture of stoicism. "Petrelli and Favero are en route. Tell me what happened."

"She died mid-interview with the Capitani reggenti not long after receiving the Order of San Marino. Surrounded by an audience of approximately a hundred and fifty, and the staff in the control room."

"I'm coming," Capparoni declared.

"Wait," I interjected. "I have Scavolini."

"Scavolini?"

" The guy who shot at me last night. Showed up again tonight. Looked like he was after La Lisa's sister, Leila."

"Leila, Marilena Lisa's sister," Capparoni echoed his sigh, a whisper of frustration. "You've certainly kept yourself busy. Listen, Luigi, don't mess with any evidence before I get there. Got it?"

"Sure."

"Should you mess with a single iota of evidence before we arrive, consider your PI license revoked."

"See you." I ended the call.

Upon my return, the reception area appeared deserted. I soon discovered the reason: the personnel had congregated in the corridor, now serving as sentinels barring entry to the studio.

I hastened to the control room, where I encountered a pair of staff members. One was armed with an iron rod, which he idly tapped against his palm.

His eyes narrowed as I approached. "Nobody's getting in or out, Signore," he announced with an edge of hostility.

I flashed my license for his scrutiny. "Police are on the way," I clarified. "Is everyone still inside?"

"Guess so," he grumbled. "A handful ran out when she collapsed, but we've kept it locked down since."

A subdued cacophony emanated from within as I entered the sanctuary of the control room. The space had transformed since my last visit: ceiling lights were ablaze, and an array of complex devices lay in various states of disassembly or repair. As I crossed the threshold, a hush fell over the room. Silvano Ghia broke the silence and approached me.

"Luigi, where the devil have you been?" He didn't pause for my response. "I can't be locked in here forever. I have a story to write, you know."

My eyes drifted to the mobile in his grasp. "Looks like you've got what you need."

His grin was self-satisfied. "I called the newsroom as soon as I heard she was dead and..."

"Who announced it from the studio?" I interjected, cutting him short.

The room grew conspicuously silent until, from behind Silvano, Furio Renzetti's voice sliced through the quiet. "Lawrence Mims was with her."

"He announced it then?"

"Yes, so what?" retorted one of the engineers, his arms crossed in a defensive posture, clearly affronted by the addition of murder to his evening's itinerary. "He held her and then yelled loud enough for everyone to hear."

My eyes scanned the room. "Who went to her after that?"

"Di Mauro," Silvano answered. "Followed by her lawyer and, naturally, the woman with the behemoth of a handbag."

I caught Renzetti's eye. "Your secretary?"

He nodded, then turned his eyes toward the door. "Signorina Serra left with Di Mauro. The rest of us stayed in this very room."

"I've never seen anything like it," said Silvano. "Damn... Imagine the headlines tomorrow!" He moved quickly, dodging a sudden, drunken swing.

"Headlines!" Franco Marini roared. "Her death is but a byline to you, isn't it? You're just a bloody scavenger!"

"Tranquillo, Marini. Take it easy," I cautioned.

Marini's eyes went wild. "To hell with you."

"I'd suggest you stay put, Marini. The police will be here soon."

"I'm not your subordinate, Ferro."

"That's abundantly clear," I retorted.

As I headed toward the door, Silvano tailed me. "A moment, Luigi! Let me get a photo of her in the studio..."

"You can get what you need through the window."

"I need a better angle!"

"Trust me, you'll soon have more angles than you bargained for."

With that, I departed. The guards positioned at the door looked inconsequentially small.

"Keep everyone inside," I instructed, leaving them to their newfound duty.

I returned to the studio, credentials in hand, for

what seemed like the umpteenth time that day. The atmosphere was dense with palpable bewilderment and grief; Marilena Lisa's final appearance on a San Marino talk show had culminated in an unthinkable tragedy. Muffled sobs and muttered conversations hummed like a dirge as I moved through the crowd.

I located Emilio Pisa, vigilant over Scavolini. Leila Luca was perched on the armrest of a nearby seat, her face a canvas of torment.

"Any trouble?" I inquired.

"None." Pisa's voice had an edge, though. "Is she really gone?"

"Yeah," I confirmed, my eyes sweeping over the hushed tableau on the studio floor. Di Mauro, flanked by a duo of SMTV employees, hovered around Marilena's now-sheeted form. Neither Mims nor Signorina Serra, Renzetti's secretary, were visible.

Leila grasped my arm. "Luigi."

"Keep it together," I advised, noting her ashen face marred by tear-streaked makeup. "The police should be here soon, and we'll be free to go."

"This is unreal. Inconceivable," she murmured.

Gently disengaging her fingers from my arm, I said, "Please, take a seat."

Redirecting my focus to Scavolini, who lay subdued on the ground, I queried, "How's our criminal guest doing?"

His glare met mine but bore no words. I observed his right arm, conspicuously limp, marred by a slowly expanding blot of dark blood.

"The police are on the way. Anything you want to say?"

"Save your breath, Sherlock." His tone was a monotonous vacuum. "Should've killed you when I had the chance."

"On your feet," I commanded.

"I'm good here," he retorted.

Ignoring his protest, I hoisted him up, inciting a sharp intake of breath as his face contorted in agony. Still, he uttered no cry. I pushed him against a nearby wall.

"Who's paying you?"

"Guess," he spat, revealing a grimy, uneven row of teeth.

"My thoughts are my own. I want to hear it from you."

"Why? If you're such a know-it-all, you can figure it out yourself," he sneered.

My knuckles found his jawline.

"Who wants Leila dead?"

"Guess," he mumbled. His eyes, dull and unfocused, betrayed a servitude to some substance—be it cocaine, cannabis, or meth. I wasn't particular about the details.

"When the Gendarmerie are done with their investigation, you'll be up for murder," I said, the solemnity of the statement hanging heavily between us.

His eyes widened, and for what felt like an age, he remained mute.

"Madness! I was just supposed to scare her—not kill her!" he finally blurted out.

"So, Marilena Lisa called you tonight, didn't she? Told you she was done with you. Getting married, moving on. That about right, Scavolini?"

His mouth opened and closed like a fish's, but no words ventured forth.

Undeterred, I pressed on, "You were backed into a corner. Couldn't go back to your old job with me and Pisa on your tail. And Marilena could ruin you, especially with her about to marry some rich guy. Right? A jury might let you slide for scaring Leila, but for killing Marilena, they'd lock you away and toss the key!"

"You're crazy!" he shrieked, lunging at me with ungoverned fury. I pushed him back, his skull colliding against the wall with a sickening thud.

"I didn't kill her. I've been here the whole time. Never even got close to Marilena."

As though I've already assembled my body of evidence, I remarked coolly, "She was poisoned. How is the drug business these days, Scavolini?"

"By God, Ferro, I didn't do it! I was just here to scare Leila, that's it."

I searched him, encountering little resistance. His wallet was heavy with banknotes. A collection of business cards occupied another pocket, a pack of cigarettes and a lighter in another. Then there was the letter, tucked into an unsealed envelope. My eyes scanned the contents briefly, recognizing the distinct script of those anonymous correspondences.

Stuffing the letter into my own pocket, I queried, "Marilena paid you to send these, didn't she?"

"She paid well," he mumbled.

"So, she wrote the letters?"

"It wasn't me, that much I can guarantee."

”Ferro, look,” Pisa interjected urgently, nodding toward the studio floor.

Officers in blue had swarmed the scene.

”Looks like the cavalry’s here,” I pronounced, looking at Scavolini one final time.

I left him leaning against the wall, his head slumping to one side. A killer who’d outlived his devil’s luck.

I found myself leaning across a table in the makeshift investigation hub, the once-bustling studio now bearing the stifling heaviness of a crime scene. Comandante Mateo Capparoni had cordoned off the area, consulting in low tones with Umberto Di Mauro and various dignitaries from SMTV. Forensic experts, donning their sterile garb, were busy dusting for prints and collecting swabs. Other uniformed officers conducted a roll call, meticulously noting the particulars of every spectator present. Enzo Scavolini had been promptly removed while Pisa conversed quietly with Leila Luca.

As I pondered my next steps, a voice broke my focus. I turned slowly. It was Silvano Ghia, the reporter.

"What should I do now?" he inquired.

"Get lost before Capparoni spots you," I advised.

"We've all been kicked out of the control room after questioning," he sighed. "The rumors circulate like wildfire. Can you clear things up?"

I offered no immediate reply. He pressed on, exasperated. "Caspita! Ferro, you must understand the magnitude of this for me."

"Why so?" I inquired.

"Because this is seismic—the most riveting event since the Mafia Capitale expose. Who would want Marilena Lisa dead?"

"Could be anyone," I offered indifferently.

”Scorned lovers? Jilted husbands? What of Lawrence Mims?”

”He conveniently pulled some strings and got himself out of here,” I revealed.

Silvano whistled softly. ”That won't sit well with the police.”

”They know where to find him,” I said. ”Is Renzetti out there among the crowd?”

”Indeed. They're in the reception area. But the pale-faced secretary is missing. Do you think she did it?”

”Give it a rest, Silvano,” I commented.

”People are whispering Marilena was poisoned. Do you think she took something before going on stage, and it got switched? What say you, Luigi?”

”You're full of theories,” I chuckled.

”Do you know what's about to happen?” Silvano lamented. ”A media horde will descend upon us, cameras ablaze. And here I am, trapped—” He trailed off, dabbing his plump face with a handkerchief. ”Damn, I could use a stiff drink.”

”Go ahead.”

He reached for a glass near a carafe along the wall.

”Sometimes, one must lower oneself to mere water.” As he poured, I slapped his wrist. The glass tumbled toward the table's edge; I caught it just in time.

”Are you mad, Ferro?” Silvano bellowed. All eyes turned toward us as the law in the form of Capparoni approached, his stride unfaltering.

”What's going on?” he queried.

I held my tongue.

Capparoni's gaze shifted from me to Silvano and

the water carafe. "I just wanted some water," Silvano simpered.

"Or perhaps you wanted to destroy evidence?" I countered.

"Evidence?" Silvano scoffed, turning to Capparoni. "Comandante, a statement if you—"

His blunder was unambiguous. Capparoni interjected: "You are media, I presume?"

"Silvano Ghia, correspondent for La Tribuna Oggi. So, your thoughts—"

"Leave. Now," Capparoni cut him off, terse yet unyielding.

"But surely—"

"Go to the reception area, Signor Ghia."

Silvano sought to remonstrate.

"Please, Comandante. I have an obligation to inform the public."

Capparoni's reply was courteously icy. "Your duty is getting in the way. Leave until we say you can come back."

Silvano cast a venomous look at Capparoni, muttered a string of incomprehensible words under his breath, and stalked off. The Comandante then pivoted to face me.

"That decanter," I said, gesturing, "Marilena Lisa drank from it just before her interview."

His nod was a slow, considered motion. "I should have thought of it myself. You stood here by the table like a guard on duty."

Pivoting again, Capparoni's voice rose, sharp and succinct: "Favero!" A burly detective, garbed in a conspicuously cheap, gray polyester suit, detached himself from the forensic huddle around Marilena's lifeless form. He shot a cursory glance in my direction before focusing his attention on the Comandante.

"You called, Comandante?"

"Take that jug and glass to Forensics. Check for prints and analyze the water."

Favero nodded solemnly and set about his task.

"Let's get some fresh air," Capparoni said, breathing heavily.

We traversed the double doors, exiting into a corridor. "We can talk in Di Mauro's office," he stated, leading the way with an air of proprietorship as if he'd always belonged in the labyrinthine bowels of SMTV.

Once inside, he left the door ajar and settled into Di Mauro's lavishly appointed chair. Fingers finding the right contact on the screen, he made a call. "Chief, Capparoni here."

The office was large and tastefully decorated, with a glass door connecting directly to the main studio. Di Mauro had fastened it securely when I'd raised the alert before the police's arrival. An additional window offered a view into a smaller, adjacent studio. Across the room, three expansive screens adorned the wall.

Capparoni ended his call, debriefing evidently complete. He rose from the desk and stared at me. "You always find trouble, don't you, Luigi?"

His gaze shifted beyond the glass door, gesturing at a gray-haired man clad in an antiquated, wrinkled suit. The man stood talking to a uniformed officer. Catching the officer's eye, he subtly nudged the older man. Acknowledging Capparoni's wave, the man began moving toward the door.

As I unfastened and pushed open the door, Capparoni introduced him. "I don't believe you've had the pleasure. Ferro, meet our newly-appointed forensic physician, Dottore Benedetto, formerly of Rome."

"Nice to meet you, Luigi Ferro," Benedetto said, nodding curtly before turning back to Capparoni.

"It's fairly straightforward," he said.

"Well, don't keep us in suspense. Spill it," Capparoni commanded.

"Potassium cyanide. No doubt about it. The scent is inescapable," Benedetto declared, his eyes narrowing.

"Fast-acting, isn't it?" I queried.

"Practically instantaneous. She might have had a capsule in her mouth and bitten down."

"Any evidence of glass in her mouth?" I pressed.

Benedetto's eyes sharpened at the question. "None that I've seen. Are you implying she didn't take it willingly?"

"I see no motivation for suicide," I said, swiveling towards Capparoni. "This evening, she was due to announce her engagement to Lawrence Mims."

"The finance magnate? Di Mauro mentioned that he left quickly. I've dispatched a car to collect him from his hotel." Capparoni's gaze shifted back to Benedetto. "How could one covertly administer potassium cyanide?"

Benedetto shrugged. "Could be a lot of ways, but a capsule would be tricky."

"What about dissolving it in her water? Say, in her drinking water?" I interrupted.

"Ferro was present at the moment of her collapse,"

Capparoni clarified. "He saw her sip the water right before she keeled over."

"A few minutes passed between her drinking and her collapse. Would that timeline fit for potassium cyanide poisoning?"

"Most likely," conceded Benedetto. "The time would depend on the concentration of the poison in the water."

"Wouldn't she have tasted the bitterness?"

Benedetto shrugged once more. "Perhaps, but there are documented instances where victims haven't. How much did she drink, Ferro?"

"Enough to wet her mouth initially, followed by a more generous swallow. No more than that."

"You can remove the body now, Dottore," Capparoni ordered. "Ensure forensics have what they need."

"I'll have her in the lab within the half-hour. You'll have a report by daybreak," Benedetto affirmed.

"Before you go," I interjected as Benedetto turned to leave. "Consider this: Marilena Lisa was a professional TV host, an artist on the verge of national recognition. Coupled with her impending engagement announcement, the stakes for her were sky-high. Under such stress, she might easily have missed the water's bitter taste."

"Could be," Benedetto agreed. Capparoni nodded.

"My work revolves around facts," Benedetto said, a sly smile crossing his lips. "You, Signori, can figure out what she was thinking and why."

With a final nod, he took his leave.

"He's seldom wrong. If he says it's potassium cyanide, then it is," Capparoni declared. "The rapid action suggests she ingested it minutes before collapsing."

"You're testing the water, right?"

"Of course. Our labs can operate with speed when the situation calls for it."

At that moment, Favero poked his head through the door. "The audience. We've collated names, addresses, and their reasons for attending. What now?"

Capparoni looked at me pensively. "Someone in that crowd could be guilty. But for now, let them go, Favero."

I pulled out the anonymous letter I'd confiscated from Scavolini, laying it on the desk.

"I have more to tell you, Capparoni," I announced, my eyes meeting his.

*

I bore witness to the initial interrogations ensconced in the shadowy contours of the makeshift questioning room. Comandante Mateo Capparoni had claimed Di Mauro's sanctum as his impromptu headquarters. Outside its door, a uniformed officer assumed a sentry's stiff posture. Beyond the glass door, the studio sprawled in twilight, occasionally punctuated by the movement of men in fluorescent orange vests. They'd finally taken Marilena Lisa's lifeless form away on a stretcher. The throng of audience members had been dismissed; office staff, too, had vacated the scene.

A sepulchral silence had descended upon the space, a somber contrast to the preceding bedlam. I reclined against the room's rear wall, Favero flanking me like a sentinel.

Seated behind the borrowed desk was Comandante Capparoni, his unflappable demeanor in place. On the desk's far corner, Petrelli—the junior officer on the scene—had discreetly positioned his recording device, never lifting his eyes during the interviews.

"Please, have a seat, Signor Di Mauro," Capparoni offered, his voice imbued with a respectful gravitas.

Umberto Di Mauro, however, his distinguished silver mane mussed and his alabaster shirt gaping at the collar, retorted with a rigid fervor, "This is ridiculous, Comandante. I must protest!"

Capparoni merely cast him a permissive look. "Against what, Signor Di Mauro?"

"This inquisition! My own producer was subjected to this for over ten minutes."

"Indeed," Capparoni interjected, not unkindly. "The producer provided invaluable insights into the layout and logistics of a television recording. These inquiries are necessary, Signor Di Mauro. It's part of the job."

"Mio Dio! Not my job! The media swarm—the flashing bulbs, the reporters—"

"They have been shooed away, Signor Di Mauro. But that's what happens when there's a murder."

Di Mauro seemed to age a decade in that instant; his practiced air of sophistication vanished. "Fine, let's get this over with, Comandante."

"Excellent. Shall we commence then? Take a seat."

Di Mauro lowered himself onto the chair's edge with palpable reluctance, perched as if ready to flee.

Capparoni reviewed the notes before him. "How long did you know Marilena Lisa?"

"Five or six years."

"She was under contract with you?"

"I thought the producer had briefed you."

"Kindly respond with a yes or a no, Signor Di Mauro."

"Yes! Yes, and this mess is going to cost me a million euros!" Di Mauro's eyes darted toward me before he cast them down, defeated.

"How well did you know her outside of work?"

"We were close. Very close."

"How close?"

The question ignited a flicker of indignation in Di Mauro. "That's personal, Comandante."

"Murder doesn't care about personal boundaries. So, just friends or what?"

"She was a close friend, nothing more."

"Did you know she was getting married? "

The color drained and then bloomed again on Di Mauro's visage. "I do now."

"Would her marriage have pleased you?"

"Not really."

Di Mauro made a feeble attempt to rally, his eyes once again seeking me out. "Look, I cared about her. If she wanted to marry Mims, who am I to stop her?"

"What about her financial situation?"

Di Mauro bristled. "She was doing fine, didn't need anyone's money."

"So, she wasn't marrying for money?"

Di Mauro's eyes narrowed at Capparoni. But he said nothing, his silence speaking volumes.

Di Mauro emitted a laugh, brittle as shattered glass. "Look, she had her own money, Comandante. She was financially secure, not to the extent of Mims, mind you, who has fortunes. You'd be wasting your time with the gold-digging theory."

"And yet," Capparoni mused, "the marriage would have been something of an achievement for Signora Lisa? A social triumph?"

The disdain was nearly palpable as Di Mauro shot back, "If that's how you want to put it, sure. Mims is a catch."

Scribbling briefly on his notepad, Capparoni pressed on. "Franco Marini—was he in the studio before the broadcast?"

"Marini? I don't think so."

"He was seen with you in the control room."

"True, but I can't say where he was before that. I was too busy in the control room to look for him."

Di Mauro shifted his gaze toward me. "Ferro, you saw me bring you into the control room, right?"

"Precisely," I confirmed.

"So, you could've gone into the studio before the show started?"

"I guess, but I never needed to. Only the crew and audience were there during the show," he finalized.

"Si," Capparoni acknowledged. I took the opportunity to interject.

"May I ask a question? Do you know when the water carafe was put in the studio?"

"Ask the producer or crew. I don't deal with small stuff like that," Di Mauro retorted.

"We've asked. But nobody seems to remember. I hoped you would know."

"I am not involved with such details," he quipped, "that's what staff are for."

"Very well. You can go," Capparoni said.

Di Mauro rose, his face a mask of palpable relief. However, he paused. "What killed Marilena?"

"Poison," Capparoni stated without inflection.

With that, Di Mauro exited, his steps laden with an unspoken weight.

Favero cleared his throat, disrupting the silence. "Next up is the lawyer, Furio Renzetti. Should we talk to the tech crew, too?"

"Get their statements and let them go," Capparoni instructed.

Favero murmured to the officer by the door before reclaiming his seat. In walked Furio Renzetti, ignoring my presence altogether.

"Furio Renzetti," he announced. "I'm not saying anything without legal representation."

Capparoni reclined, fingertips meeting in a contemplative steeple. "Signor Renzetti, thank you for coming. Relax, this is just a chat. You're not being forced to talk."

"Good to know," Renzetti said, his smile steeped in irony as he continued to stand, refusing the chair offered to him.

"Let's discuss your acquaintance with the deceased. She was a friend?"

"We were good friends," the lawyer replied.

"And her circle? Did you know her other friends?"

"Some of them."

"What about her enemies?"

The question hung heavy, unanswered, filling the room like a slowly spreading fog.

A somber quiet enveloped the room before Renzetti broke it. "Marilena didn't have enemies. Everyone loved her. She was universally adored."

Capparoni's lean face remained inscrutable as he responded, "You served as legal counsel to Signora Lisa. Why are you here tonight?"

"She invited me. Said she had big news to share after the show."

"And you have no idea what it was?"

"Not a clue."

I seized the opportunity to interject. "Your secretary had a chat with Franco Marini. He told her that Marilena was going to announce an engagement. You really didn't know?"

His eyes locked onto mine, flaring with indignant surprise. "Engagement? My secretary and I don't exchange romantic gossip."

"Where's your secretary now?"

"Pardon?"

"Signorina Serra, your secretary. Where is she?"

"She felt sick when she heard about Marilena. Last I heard, she was recovering in the reception area."

Capparoni glanced at Favero, who gave a subtle shake of his head.

"So, where is she?" I pressed.

"I don't know. I'm not her babysitter."

"How long has she worked for you?" I asked.

"Comandante Capparoni," Renzetti pivoted towards him, "must I endure this scrutiny? From him?"

"Maybe you find it less taxing to answer me," Capparoni rejoined. "How about Signorina Serra's employment?"

His response was charged with vexation. "Why do you care about her? She's been with me for ten years, maybe more."

"She hails from Puglia, quite close to Marilena Lisa's roots, does she not?" I added.

Renzetti paused before admitting, "Yes, I think she's from Puglia."

"Did you know about Marilena's past?" Capparoni inquired.

"Naturally."

"Did you know she had a sister, Leila Luca?"

His hesitance was palpable, but finally, he conceded, "Yes. I knew."

He suddenly lunged forward. "Leila killed her! She hated Marilena! And that was no secret. She tried to bleed her sister dry!"

"Do you have proof to back up such an allegation?"

The room descended into another weighty silence.

"I have blackmail letters in my office safe," he finally replied.

"I trust you'll bring them to the Gendarmerie tomorrow. And how do you know Leila wrote them?"

"I don't need proof. I'm sure of it."

"That's an interesting way to think for a lawyer," Capparoni remarked just as a phone trilled in the background. Petrelli answered discreetly and covered the mouthpiece.

"Comandante, it's for you."

Capparoni received the phone with an air of finality. "We are done now, Signor Renzetti. You can leave."

As the door closed behind the irritated lawyer, I turned my attention to officer Favero.

"Signorina Joana Serra—she's not here anymore, is she?"

"Can't say she is. You think something's up?"

"Do you have her address."

"It's in the files. She wasn't in the reception when we got here, by the way."

Favero was interrupted by a subtle cue from an officer by the door. He excused himself, making his exit as Capparoni returned from his call.

"Lab results, Ferro. You hit the mark. The water contained potassium cyanide."

Favero reentered. "Lawrence Mims is here."

"Stall him. Bring Franco Marini to me."

Marini walked in, his complexion ghostly. "Sorry for being rude earlier. Marilena's death messed me up."

"You were married to her?" Capparoni asked, not unkindly.

"For four turbulent years," Marini clarified, wiping his brow with his sleeve. " If you think I killed her, you're wrong. I loved that woman—every strand of her hair."

Capparoni raised a transcript sheet. "You said you were in the control room. Two people back you up. Anything you wish to add?"

"Only that I wish I could find her killer myself," Marini retorted.

Just then, a commotion erupted at the door, and in barreled Lawrence Mims, flushed and furious. "This is an outrage! Manhandling me here? I'm filing a complaint first thing tomorrow!"

Catching Capparoni's eye, I rose and motioned to Favero. We stepped outside.

"Mims thinks he owns the place," Favero huffed.

"Favero, I need that address for Joana Serra."

"You've got it, but—"

"Tell Capparoni I'll be in touch."

Moments later, I was weaving through the nocturnal streets, my Vespa humming beneath me. In my head, the thoughts were humming a different tone. Two sisters from humble beginnings in the south of Italy. Both wrote to the other with demands and threats. One was killed, and the other escapes the same faith by pure luck—three times. There must be a third party involved, and it was to that address I steered my motor.

10

Tucked away on an inscrutable cul-de-sac, she dwelled in a residential building that exuded a peculiar tranquility. Its entrance was secured by an electronic lock, a modernity at odds with its otherwise antiquated visage. Forced into a patience-testing ten-minute sojourn, I finally found my entry as another tenant made his exit. Ascending a pair of staircases, worn from years of routine footfall, I navigated down an elongated hallway until I came to knock upon the door at its terminus. It opened promptly, though only enough to reveal the tenant through a safety chain's constraint.

"Signorina Serra?" I asked.

"Si, I figured you'd show up."

"I'm just here to talk. Can I come in?"

"You're wasting your time, Signor Ferro," she quipped, her voice crystalline but devoid of fervor.

"It's late, but not too late for a chat. How about it?"

As I added, "Would you rather talk to Capparoni's uniformed men?" I heard the sibilance of her sigh.

"Fine, whatever," she resigned, the chain relinquishing its duty as she allowed me entry.

"Benvenuto, Signor Ferro," she greeted me, pulling the door closed with a gentle click. My eyes surveyed the room, softly illuminated by a pair of lamps—one of which possessed the character of a votive, casting its glow on a portrait of a man. Furio Renzetti.

"Yes, I've had a crush on Renzetti for years," she

declared from behind me in a voice marked by restraint. "But he never noticed."

Something in her timbre compelled me to spin around. She was armed, her grip on the firearm unyielding.

"Whoa, easy there," I urged. "Put the gun down, Signorina Serra."

Her head made a languid motion of denial, her eyes revealing a sort of desolate void.

"You figured it out, didn't you? I killed her, I did. Now I have to kill you too. You're too smart for your own good. I wrote those letters, faking Leila's handwriting. Got them to turn on each other, Marilena's life turned into a living inferno—quite the success, wouldn't you agree?"

As she prattled on, I discretely edged closer, foot by foot.

"In believing Leila, the blackmailer, Marilena revealed her own sordid self," she continued, relishing her recount. "Marilena even tried to kill her sister with poisoned chocolates. That was the best part."

Her laughter tinkled through the air, a sound incongruously youthful and one that sent a disconcerting shiver down my spine.

"Those chocolates were my idea. Filled them with potassium cyanide myself. Got Marilena to commit attempted murder. Funny, right? She even hired Scavolini, a guy from her druggie days." She paused to savor her own wit.

As she rambled, her gun arm lowered an inch or two. I took the opportunity to advance cautiously.

"The irony? Scavolini failed, and Leila lived on,

haunted by Marilena's poisoned letters. My true genius was always in the shadows. Not even Renzetti suspected anything," she continued, her eyes momentarily losing focus as though riveted by some imagined spectacle on the ceiling. "Renzetti had no idea what Marilena was capable of. But I knew. Because I'm clever."

"You thought Marilena was gonna get engaged to Renzetti tonight, didn't you?" I interrupted. "That was the breaking point for you."

"Ah, Signor Ferro," she sank briefly, then straightened up with a brightening visage. "It nearly crushed me. But I knew what I had to do: Marilena had to die."

"You followed the girl with the water into the studio, slipping cyanide into Marilena's glass?"

"Correct, Signor Ferro. And the girl who helped me without knowing? Gave her a chocolate as a thank-you."

My eyes followed her glance toward the bulky handbag on the side table. A repository of deadly sweets. I lunged.

The gunshot echoed off the walls as plaster from the ceiling rained down around us. She let out an ear-piercing scream and stumbled into my arms, her limbs shaking with fear. I wrenched the gun from her grip and flung it across the room in one fluid motion. Her body crashed hard onto the floor as her eyes fluttered shut. I knelt beside her, watching her shallow breaths as she lay motionless.

"Signor Ferro..." she wheezed.

I wrapped my hands around her and dragged her to an armchair, squeezing her into it until she seemed immobilized. I felt a panic rising as I saw the extent of her breakdown. Snapping out of it, I reached for my phone when suddenly I heard a sound. I whipped around and saw Joana Serra fiddling with her bag's lock on the sideboard. Instantly, I dropped the phone and sprinted across the room, but it was too late. She had already shoveled chunks of chocolate into her mouth like a ravenous animal. I grabbed her and jerked her body so that our eyes met. Desperate thoughts of antidotes, emetics, and doctors flooded my mind.

But I realized it was too late.

"Would you care for a chocolate, Signor Ferro?" Her words slurred as her head lolled to one side, neck slackening as though its support had been cut. Her dark locks framed a face that seemed suddenly ancient, sapped of youth and vitality.

Old, very old. And withered. And lifeless.

*

"We thought you'd find your way back to the studio," Leila said, her voice tinged with a lament. "We all waited for what felt like ages."

"The night's drama is over, Leila," I returned, eyeing the periphery. Emilio Pisa loomed in the doorway, his face etched with solemnity as his eyes seemed to penetrate the obsidian darkness outside. "Nice meeting you."

"But Luigi—"

"I must make a call," I interrupted, placing my hand gently upon her delicate shoulder. "May you find peace, especially at home."

I swiveled away, fishing my mobile out. She remained a spectral presence behind me, a wisp of unvoiced expectations. With no further preamble, I dialed.

"Caterina, darling," I announced with a clarity intended more for Leila than the impending call.

I heard her footsteps receding before the first ring had ended. Glancing up, I watched as Leila Luca vanished through the doorway, Emilio Pisa's arm as her chosen escort.

"Luigi, my love! I've been so worried," Caterina's voice enveloped me through the phone, breathy with expectation. "I've seen the news about Marilena—so where are you now?"

"Still at the office. But I'm wrapping up to head home."

"You shouldn't, you know."

"What?"

"Go home. I'm waiting for you, Luigi," she said, her voice almost tactile, vibrating through the receiver and resonating in my palm. "Don't keep me waiting for long."

I didn't. Forgetting the frayed edges of the day, forgetting the night steeped in tension and unspooled narratives, I simply allowed myself to forget.

THE END

LUIGI FERRO
WILL RETURN

A Story from

Yesteryear's Stories Reflected Today
Yabot AB
www.yabot.se

www.ingramcontent.com/pod-product-compliance
Lightning Source LLC
LaVergne TN
LVHW020339200726
843507LV00012B/2422